KEEPERS OF THE BRIDGE

IMMORTAL BELOVED

ALAIN LOUIS CAMUS

Copy-editing – Mr Neville Shaw
Final proof – Micheline François
Cover Design and Layout – Arjan van Woensel

Library of Congress Cataloguing-in-Publication Data
ISBN paperback 978-0-6457676-7-4
ISBN e-book 978-0-6457676-8-1

Alain Francois
PO Box 22 St Marys TAS 7215
alainlouiscamus@gmail.com

Publisher
阿蘭

A catalogue record for this work is available
from the National Library of Australia.

BOOKS BY
ALAIN LOUIS CAMUS

Book One

The Tears of Apphat, Immortal Beloved

Book Two

Silence of the Stars,

Chronicles of Azizi

Book Three

Keepers of the Bridge,

Chronicles of Azizi

Book Four

Aïschah Silver Moon

Language of the Stars

DEDICATION AND ACKNOWLEDGEMENT

To my Great Grandmother Alice Camus for always being by my side, encouraging me and guiding me throughout this journey.

My mother, Blanche for her unfailing support and encouragement.

To all my readers
You know who you are.
No matter how close or how far,
Thank you for reading my stories,
the journey and the emotions
you shared with me.

Balduh-Shtar
Asfaine Mountains
The Kingdom of Gleskerell
Cave of Gibrar
The Giants Steps
Naassée
Isthmus of Mina
The Great Marshlands
Dessert of Keyar
Oasis of Shahreza
The Huda Pass
Ocean of Malkizar
Ocean of Elwah
Schiraz

In a land that is not on any of your maps, a culture based on ancient Lore beyond your understanding, in a language that is barely able to be translated into yours, I exist. My name is Azizi, it means Beloved in the ancient tongue of the Desert People. I will be known as the Immortal Beloved.

PROLOGUE

Of Aïschah Healer and Magician
Respected Elder of the Council of Naasée.
Godmother to Aldrick, later known as Azizi – the beloved

Twenty-two years ago, *Aïschah*, powerful healer and magician, one of the greatest seer and star caster, had drawn her own star chart, prompted by a dream brought to her by *Caelesti*, the wife of the village chief *Haakon*. Caelesti is an enigma, she came from a distant village at the foot of the Asfaine mountains on the edge of the Great Desert of Keyab. Aïschah soon realised that Caelesti had obviously inherited the second sight. The dream she brought to Aïschah, echoed the star chart, announcing the birth of a child of exceptional powers, which suggested the fulfilment of a prophecy of one who would recover the Sacred Tears of Apphat. But the star chart also hinted at a death – this aspect has haunted Aïschah for years. The conclusion of her chart asserted that she had at best twenty-two years to accomplish her life's work. Prompted by *Prince Elwah*, she made the reluctant decision to take on an apprentice. Soon, a rumour spread that she was training a young man into the ways of healing and magic. She had named him Azizi, meaning 'Beloved'. His unique ability as a healer was spreading quickly amongst mountain villagers.

Of Elwah
Prince of Naasée

Prince Elwah, so named for his responsibility as the Keeper or Haafiz of the Sacred Tear, 'Elwah' of Apphat. His place secured as the apparent reincarnation of the previous Haafiz, determined by the intensity of his blue eyes and extraordinary magical ability. *Elwah* quickly became the most powerful magicians in the kingdom of *Balduh-Shtar*. However, his title as Prince and Haafiz of Elwah, is being challenged by enemies within the Council of Elders, jealous of his authority.

An adept at reading star charts, he had carefully examined the chart that *Aïschah* had brought to him. He quickly recognised that the stars at a given date would align in the north in such a way, as to confirm a prophesy long held but never clearly interpreted. It was at this point *Elwah* urged *Aïschah* to take on an apprentice. He vowed to guide and protect the child no matter what.

Of Saeed

Son of Fariqa

Saeed the beloved and only son of a desert couple from the Huda Pass, looks deeply into Azizi's eyes, and remembers how blue the sky was the day a scorpion had stung him. How blue were the eyes that suddenly appeared before him, as a young man with pale skin and jet-black hair had held his hand and spoke to his mind, telling him that all would be well, that all he had to do was to fight the poison and live. Quietly, the boy *Saeed* fell in love with his rescuer, never imagining that one day fate would bring them together. Fond of the fragrance of orange blossoms that reminds him of his Yumma – his maternal grandmother.

Of Prince Ijlal

Heir to the kingdom of Schiraz

The anticipation of a first-born male gave way to a great deal of celebration at the birth of Prince *Ijlal* to Sultan *Maltiza and his wife* of Schiraz. However, born at the start of season of Malkizar, the royal star casters had warned of possible difficulties that the prince would face during his late adolescence. The fact that the prince's mother died shortly after giving birth only added a grief and a strong desire for the Sultan to protect his only son.

Despite one individual star caster foretelling a royal partnership, and the protection from the greatest magician since King Apphat's rule, the prince would be the target of political plots and attempted assassination.

The Sultan *Maltiza* appointed his own brother, *Giafar* as the protector of the prince. The Sultan took further steps to protect his only son. As soon as he could walk and swing a sword, the best swordsmen in the land were given the tasks of training his son in self-defence. One instructor, *Hasan* taught Ijlal not only the art of defence and offence, but the flexibility and speed required to achieve total control through arduous exercises of suppleness and speed. Hasan came from Naasée, renowned for their fearless soldiers.

Ijlal proved to be a natural, even inventing moves and counter moves that flowed smoothly and too quick even for the most astute observer. One such move involved changing his sword from his dominant hand to the other so swiftly that it confused the opponent.

Still concerned at the predictions of possible political plots, Ijlal's father, the sultan advised his son to befriend every eldest son in the kingdom and form his own private army, train them in the skills that he had acquired and swear them to absolute fealty. Thus 'The *Companions*' as they came to be known was formed; their reputation grew far and wide for their sense of justice for the people and their skill and fearlessness in battle. *Faruq*, Ijlal's cousin and son to the king's brother *Giafar* became Ijlal's most ardent follower and was named by prince Ijlal as Captain of the Royal guards.

Following a prophetic dream that no one could interpret, Ijlal went with his uncle Giafar to consult the famed Seeress *Aïschah*. Her presence as a powerful magician and healer impressed him but it was a young man with piercing blue eyes, pale skin and jet-black hair that stunned him; especially when this young man, named *Azizi* spoke with the power of the Great Spirit. His immediate thought was, *when I reach the throne in my father's place, I want this man by my side, always.*

Of General Faruq
Cousin to prince Ijlal

Personal bodyguard and captain of the royal army to Ijlal, his cousin; third in line to the throne of Schiraz. Fierce soldier endowed with piercing blue eyes and an attitude to match the meaning of his name: *one who distinguishes truth from falsehood.*

Devoted to protecting his cousin, Prince Ijlal. *Faruq* possesses the terrifying skills of a determined soldier who took on the training of the sons of nobles and helped form the small army known as 'The Companions'.

Of The Companions
Protectors of Schiraz

The Companions made up of the first-born sons of the nobility numbered seven in all. Each with a name that very accurately describes a trait of their personality, something *Faruq* a year older than the prince, understood and developed those attributes, encouraged them as part of a strategy for all occasions.

Most of the companions were either the same age or younger than the prince.

The twins *Rauf* and *Isamadeen* soon joined. The Companions soon learned that *Rauf,* whose name means gentle and kind and with a baby face to match that inspired immediate trust, was as fierce a fighter as any of them. A personality and trait that Faruq exploited on many occasions to win the upper hand.

His brother *Isamadeen,* although a twin born a few minutes before would often remind him that as the eldest, it was still his responsibility to pull his brother back into line. Always done with good humour, Isamadeen's name in the ancient language of the desert people means to 'guard', equipped with an attitude of readiness and focussed attention. Strangers who were not as familiar with the twins, would always approach them with caution.

The rest of the Companions, Husam, Fatin and Jamal make up the small but effective army that *Azizi* once described as one of the swiftest most ruthless attacks he had ever seen. Their eventual defeat of the guards of the Overlord and the Red Robes protecting the Sorceress, became a tale of adventure told to the young and old alike. It was told so many times that it eventually grew into legend.

Of Master Sahir

One of the Elders on the Council of Naasée, mage for the Huda People, He is reputed to be one hundred years old. He promises *Saeed* to reveal his paternal heritage.

Of Aldrick, known as Azizi,

Seer and Prophet of Apphat – Immortal beloved.

Godson to Aïschah

Bullied at school, haunted by visions he did not understand and the ability to foresee events that confounded him, made him a target of ridicule amongst the students at the temple school of Asfaine. Labelled as a daydreamer by his teacher, *Delenna Tobba-ha* one of the few female teachers at the temple school.

Friend of the shepherds of the village of Asfaine and secretly protected by them, his power of clairvoyance enables him to communicate with nature spirits and find potent herbs in secret places that most people would not know of.

Eventually *Aïschah* takes him away from the toxic environment of school and promises to train him in the ways of healing and magic. His abilities soon exceed her expectations, bewildering and leaving her with a sense of disquiet.

I place my hand on his heart, I take his hand and place it on mine, and I ask him, "Saeed, what is in here, what do you feel?" At once he opens his eyes wide. The uncertainty leaves him.

We both intone each with our own voice,

"May my heart and days of light embrace you. May that love inside of you fly with wings. Magic is within you, let it flow into and from you."

The wind in the chamber suddenly roars with the rage of a thousand beasts, the waters around us tear at us, some drops so sharp that they cut deep into our flesh. Droplets of blood mix with the water, all appears to be lost. We are not separate, we are one! With all my might, calling on all the power within me, I pronounce:

"Ap! Phat!"

The world suddenly stands still. The waters freeze in place. Two lights of the purest blue manifest between us. Two voices in unison command, "Joy and Sorrow cannot one with the other be. Choose!"

CHAPTER ONE

The sheer power and authority in my voice is unmistakable. With the command of the Sacred words of Incantation pronounced, the world holds its breath.

The simplicity of the Incantation, the power behind it, has left all the Elders bewildered; except for my godmother, who is beaming with pride. *Yes! The king has two names!*

The mage for the Huda people, Mahjir Sahir's voice gilded with humour acknowledges, "Of course! The shortest and most powerful spell is a name. In this case two names of power!" Regaining a little of his composure, he does not hold back his mirth of admiration.

Everyone in the cave of the Calling heard the Twin voices clear as bells, ordering Saeed and I to choose one of the Sacred Stone.

A dark cloud of greed insinuates itself around Saeed, as Master Ahmad's voice heard by all present, orders Saeed, "Boy, you must take both, one is of no use!"

There is no turning back for any of us. Ahmad's statement heard by all, will seal his fate. Now Saeed and I must step forward and choose. My heart is pounding in my chest, the significance of the moment is overwhelming. This time I am bound to choose a stone and not have it passed on to me from anyone. The sudden sense of responsibility makes me hesitate. My hands are by my side, unsure which stone I should take. Perhaps, if I let Saeed choose first then my task will be easier, I will take the remaining Sapphire regardless of which it is.

You were chosen! You were born to this task and trained for it many lifetimes ago!

The voice, unambiguous in its authority, resonates in my head and suddenly fills my heart. My chest expands, my back straightens, I recognise the importance of the choice I am about to make; in silence I bow to the wisdom spoken and consciously regain the confidence I have denied for so long. A part of me, the darkest part of me, recognises the light of my training and finally understands the reason I hid my pain as doubt for so long.

My hand reaches out and without further thought or denial I clasp the Sacred Sapphire that glows with the light of my mountain sky in mid-summer, the Sacred Sapphire of Elwah. A flow of warm energy begins to course through my arm and body, flooding my entire being. Every spell I have ever learned, every piece of knowledge for healing is suddenly made vivid in my mind, a sense of enrichment fills me; my body, my mind and my spirit are suddenly energised. At the very same moment, I watch as Saeed clasps his hand over the stone that glows the deep blue of the ocean, patterned with floating islands of teal, occasionally crisscrossed with bolts of pure white; he takes the Sacred Sapphire of Malkizar.

The cave is suddenly plunged into darkness, only the slight glimmer of the sapphires throws shards of light that bounce around the walls. All the torches in the cavern have been extinguished with a single gust of wind.

Saeed and I look at each other. His face has changed. There is a subtle light within that shines through his eyes. His beautiful emerald green eyes have taken a deeper hue, occasionally sparkling with the faintest dark teal of the deep ocean. Truly his eyes have become magical.

Saeed is looking at me with awe. He smiles and whispers, "Azizi, I can see the whole sky in your eyes!"

Smiling back, "and I can see all the oceans in yours."

The walls of water have thinned but still stand between the Elders and us. A light begins to form within the water and a silhouette appears, taking on a mixture of the light of the sapphires, strands of golden light emanating through the veil of water. A woman appears, indistinct at first then takes on the features of the woman we witnessed in Elwah's memories. With great reverence, I recognise the Goddess Ishtar as she manifests between Saeed and me.

With a murmur that radiates joy, she speaks directly to our minds. The words are like the sounds of nature, the whispering breeze in tall grass, the soft gurgle of my mountain streams, the wind as it flows over the sand dunes of the desert of Keyab; the words are a command, and she instructs us to repeat them.

Saeed and I, each holding the sacred sapphire we chose, raise it to just below our heart and repeating the words Ishtar pronounces, the Sacred Stones begin to glow and radiate a pure light that seems to penetrate my chest. I sense that Saeed is experiencing the same thing.

The Sapphires gradually take on a translucence without losing any of their quality of colour. With a sound like a quick intake of breath, and the last words spoken, the sapphire dissolves into my chest. I watch as the one Saeed is holding also dissolves into his being.

Ishtar speaks a final instruction to our minds: *you will no longer need to swallow the sacred stone; its essence is now within you. Its power is at your call and will be manifested with the words you have just spoken. This is necessary to protect the Sacred Sapphires. When the time comes for your body to die, the stone will simply vanish and return to me.*

The veil of water around us turns to mist and Ishtar disappears.

We are back in the cave of the Calling. Only the occasional sound of dripping water cuts through the silence.

My godmother is at my shoulder and Mahjir Sahir stands beside Saeed.

A collective sigh of relief is heard, Elwah calmly states, "The Calling ritual is complete."

"You have done well, both you." My god mother is looking at me with all the pride and admiration a teacher and a parent could have for its child. "Now, Azizi come with me and Saeed, go with Mahjir Sahir. We must ensure that you are both taken care of and safe at least for the next day."

I follow my godmother in hushed silence. Sahir with Saeed next to him follow us closely. Some of the Elders are smiling in acknowledgement, one or two stare in deference. Although Master Ahmad is smiling and nods his head, I detect an energy of barely suppressed anger.

I thought at first that we would be heading back to Hasan's

residence and the room that Saeed and I share. We reach the top of the stairs that is the secret way to the chamber of the Calling and exit the small temple. It is night and my mind tries to adjust at the lapse of time. The air is cool, the stars are out in a clear sky, a gentle breeze blows in from the desert. Aïschah confidently steps out and leads us to a small building at the side of the temple.

"Come, we don't have much time before the Elders demand a meeting to decide what is to be done with you both."

We enter through a door that has been ornately painted with fresh runic symbols. The more prominent symbols are to ward off negative energy and there are still more complex ones to protect and conceal. I recognise Aïschah's elegant writing style.

We enter a small dark room. With one gesture and no spoken words, Aïschah conjures up a bright elf light. Saeed is by my side; he slips his hand into mine and I tighten my fingers around his. Mahjir Sahir is right behind us and closes the door. He draws in the air several more sigils of protection that appear as small flames, which dissolve themselves into the wooden door.

Aïschah lets out a deep breath.

"Godmother, what is happening? Why this secrecy?"

Aïschah looks at Sahir who nods back, adding, "It is safe. This house will not be detected."

Aïschah lets out another sigh. She smiles at me and Saeed. "You have both done so well. But now comes the real test. Both of you now hold a sacred Sapphire within you. The whole assembly of Elders witnessed that. According to legend this will give you both powers beyond your current imagination. There are those who will question Elwah's reasons for choosing such young and inexperienced magicians to hold the Sacred Sapphires." With a gloomy note in her voice she adds, "And there are those who will now envy you power." She adds with even more sadness, "Elwah's title as Haafiz of the Sacred Stone of Joy is now null and void. His hold on the Council of Elders is probably unsustainable." She pauses a moment before adding, "and probably, so is his title as prince regent of Naasée."

A lump forms in my throat. Elwah protected me even when he himself was in danger and gave me so much advice and support. I look at Saeed who pales at these words.

Sahir's deep and gentle voice cuts through the tension, "Saeed, you have nothing to fear, Aïschah and I are here to protect you both, until such time as it is safe to confront the Council."

"Sahir," my godmother interrupts, "no matter how many sigils we have placed over this house, it will eventually be discovered. We need to move to a safer place."

Sahir nods in agreement, "I agree Aïschah, but where do you suggest? We cannot go out into the town now. We will be too visible. What plan do you have?"

"I have asked general Faruq and two of his trusted soldiers to wait for us at the Cave of Gibrar."

I take a quick breath; butterflies take flight in the pit of my stomach. *The cave of Gibrar? Faruq? How? Why?"*

Sahir must have read my mind. "But how are we to get there Aïschah? We would need to cross the main town and exit through the northern gate!"

"We use 'farstep' and slip into the space between."

"But they have not been trained for this, Aïschah."

"No. As long as both of us can clearly visualise our destination, then the power that now lies within them will act as an amplifier and take us there. I will take my godson; you should take Saeed."

"Godmother?" Aïschah turns to me, seeing the dread in my eyes, she smiles with what I imagine is meant as a reassuring smile.

"Do not worry Azizi. Your time to learn this technique has come, but we do not have time to teach it to you. So, Sahir and I will cast the incantation and using our will and linking with your power of the Sapphire, we will travel to the Cave of Gibrar." She then turns to Sahir to confirm, "Sahir, have you been inside the Cave of Gibrar?"

Sahir frowns slightly, which makes me even more nervous, before he adds, "Yes, but it was many years ago."

"Here." Aïschah steps forward to Sahir and placing her hand on the side of his temple, says, "look at this image, that is where I plan to go in the Cave."

Sahir nods. "Yes, that is clear." He beckons Saeed over who is visibly shaking. Sahir takes him by the hand, smiles at him, "Relax Saeed, I will do all the work. Just keep holding my hand. Nothing bad can happen to you, you are under my protection."

Saeed looks beseechingly at me. I smile and I exaggerate a deep breath, which he imitates.

"Now Saeed, stay relaxed and simply focus on your heart. Let me know when you sense a warmth in the place where the Sapphire slipped into you."

Saeed closes his eyes for a moment, taking another deep breath, his eyes snap open, his beautiful emerald green eyes have taken on a radiance that seems to grow around him, enveloping them both in a veil of sea green mist. "There, it is warm now." Saeed barely finishes his sentence when both suddenly dissolve into thin air.

"Come, Azizi, it is our turn." Aïschah holds my hand, smiles at me, "We will do the same." I close my eyes; her skin is warm and soft. A strange and childish thought crosses my mind, I think about the last time I held my godmother's hand like this, *I was ten, I think; or was it twelve?*

I open my eyes and almost stumble on the sandy floor of the Cave of Gibrar. Faruq is at my side and holds me up. My godmother is standing next to me, examining me with her keen eyes, smiles and comments, "That was a bit of a rush Azizi, I am not used to that much power."

Saeed rushes into my arms and holds me tight. "Azizi, I am not sure I will ever get used to this."

Both Sahir and Aïschah chuckle a little.

"Azizi, are you well?" Faruq has taken a few steps back, fixes me with his penetrating gaze. Saeed releases me and turns to face Faruq.

"Umm, yes, thank you Faruq. But when, how did you get here?"

Faruq gives a short laugh, "Azizi, it seems that your existence is now creating all kinds of political turmoil. Your godmother contacted me some time ago and explained what would take place and that you may need protection. Of course, I immediately volunteered."

"And so did we." The unmistakable voices of the twins Rauf and Isamadeen manifest just behind me.

I barely turn when a movement flashes past me and I watch Saeed rush and embrace Rauf, who taken aback with the suddenness of the gesture freezes in place. I can vouch that I have never seen Rauf blush before and the sight of it almost makes me giggle.

Saeed suddenly conscious of the reaction that may have caused surprise, unwinds himself from Rauf, eyes down cast, whispers a half-hearted apology before turning to Isamadeen who willingly submits himself to a firm and slightly more restrained embrace.

Faruq is trying to suppress his amusement. "Rauf always makes that impression and effect on people." With a knowing smile, he adds, "This is the reason I use him as a decoy."

I amble over to the twins. I mean to welcome them with open arms, Isamadeen raising his eyes to meet mine, hesitates, pulls Rauf's sleeve and with a bow that takes me by surprise, eyes downcast, mutters, "Mahjir."

Rauf, at first confused, takes one look at me, his jaw drops in awe, and he too bows to me. The loneliness of power stabs me once more. This time I am determined to put an end to it. I have no doubt that the light of the Sacred Sapphire is gleaming through my eyes.

I stand back and assuming an authoritative pose, "Isamadeen, Rauf, tell me – what particular type of goat would you like me to change you into, and specifically gelded or not?"

Isamadeen and Rauf stare, paling at the idea. Saeed is the first to understand the ruse and the non-existent threat. He saunters over, places an arm around my shoulders and mischievously asks, "Azizi, will you teach me that spell? Please?" The twins take a step back and Saeed laughing raucously states, "I think Azizi would like an embrace from his brothers."

The twins frozen in their dread, relax, smiling a little and tentatively step forward into my arms. "Please Isamadeen, Rauf, never again call me by that title—it makes me feel like an old man!" The tension released I add, "It is so good to see you both again so soon. Rauf, now you have an idea how much Saeed has missed you."

Rauf blushes and so does Saeed. Isamadeen in his inimitable way ruffles his brother's curls.

"Now, please tell me what this plan is all about, why, when and whatever other detail I need to know."

The twins look to Faruq, who in turn looks to Aïschah. My godmother who has kept her distance until now and has affectionately observed the twins' welcome, walks over.

"Come Azizi, Saeed, bring your friends and sit. I will explain."

We move up the cave where there are small flat rocks in a rough circle. While we sit and wait, Master Sahir has walked to the entrance of the cave. He begins to draw in the air the sigils I saw him make in the small house earlier.

"Some time before the ceremony was agreed upon, Prince Elwah spoke to me and Master Sahir privately." Aïschah pauses, realising that this will take some time to explain, she makes a decision, "here; I will use the same mind spell that Elwah used. It will be simpler if you hear and see for yourselves." Aïschah makes a small gesture to her temple, utters a few words and my mind is immediately snatched from my control.

The room I am in is not Elwah's quarters. It is somewhere in the city of Naasée but far from the palace. The room is lit with elf lights, there are no windows. Aïschah and Master Sahir are both seated listening.

Elwah is speaking, "Aïschah, Sahir, I am concerned for the safety of both Saeed and Azizi. If the ceremony is successful and one or both are given the Sacred Sapphires, several members of the Council of Elders will seek to have control over the stones. If they cannot convince the boys to relinquish the stones for 'safe keeping', they will at least attempt to sequester the boys within Naasée, never to be allowed out of their reach." Elwah pauses a moment.

"This can only mean one thing, they will attempt as they did with me, to take them, isolate them and guard them at all costs." Elwah raises a hand at Sahir's question.

"I am aware of Master Ahmad's conflict regarding who should possess and wield the Sacred Sapphires. I know that he tried to manipulate Saeed into compliance. He did not count on Saeed's intelligence or his courage. Ahmad was also aware that if the friendship between Azizi and Saeed developed further, it would complicate things and place his scheme of separating Saeed into disarray."

Elwah turns to Aïschah adding, "fortunately, Azizi was aware of the manipulation and devised a wonderful, yet simple magical talisman of great power and protection."

Elwah stands suddenly, takes a few steps to the door of the room, listening before resuming his seat. "Aïschah, how well do you know young general Faruq of Schiraz?"

"I met him when you returned to Naasée."

"Good. I do not want to involve the Sultan of Schiraz into this affair, as it could escalate matters into another conflict between nations. If you can explain and convince Faruq of the danger that both boys will be in, inform him that they will require protection for a while, at least until the Council has met. Beyond that, I will do my utmost to ensure their ongoing protection."

"Elwah, what if the ceremony is not successful and they are unable to call the Sapphires into existence?"

"A good point Sahir. Even if the ceremony is unsuccessful, the boys will become future targets by some on the council who will want to use them for their own greed." Elwah is pensive for a moment before adding, "I have seen what Azizi is capable of, and the council members are fully aware of his power in defeating the dark Sorceress. They also fear the promise that the Guardian made to Azizi, that his time would come to possess the stones once more." Reflecting a moment, smiling at Sahir, he adds, "I have also seen the power Saeed has, even untrained, he can call the Näcken of Malkizar. It is a matter of time before the members of the Council realise that together these boys will become a force to be reckoned with. Their fear of that power will make them want to control them at all costs."

Aïschah sighs, a note of irony in her voice, "It seems that even if successful, the acquisition of the Sacred Sapphires will not result in the promised and prophesised Great Harmony."

Elwah is silent.

"I do not know all things Aïschah, but I can promise you this, the world will be a better place with these two young men in it, regardless of their possession of either Tear of Apphat."

"What do you require us to do then?" Sahir softly asks.

"Two things: first Sahir, you would have mapped Saeed's star map shortly after he was born as I requested?" Sahir nods. "Good, I would like you to share that knowledge with Aïschah. And Aïschah, I want you to compare Azizi's chart with Saeed's, I hope you will come to the same conclusion I have."

Elwah remains enigmatically silent.

"And the second?" Sahir asks quietly.

Elwah shakes himself out of a reverie, "Yes. At the conclusion of the ceremony, take Azizi and Saeed away as quickly as possible and hide them. If Faruq agrees and arrives in time with a few soldiers, they should provide protection and safe passage away from Naasée. I will not tell you where, nor will I seek to know – the less I know when I address Council the better."

The mind link with Aïschah is suddenly cut and with a slight lurch, I find myself back in the cave of Gibrar. Faruq, Isamadeen and Rauf still mesmerised by the power of the mind link, stare into space in awe at the experience.

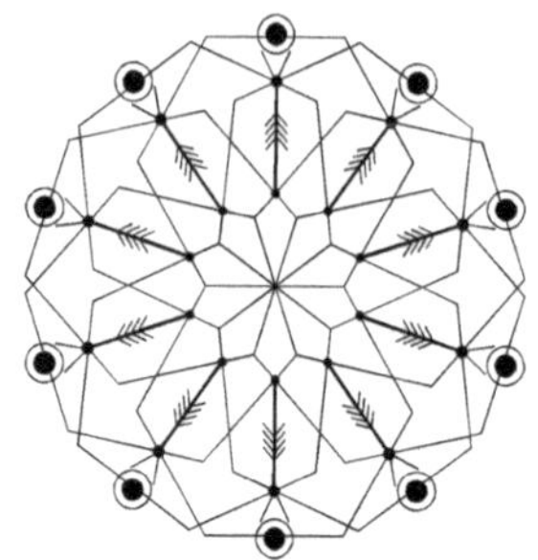

CHAPTER TWO

The silence of the cave is cold and oppressive. A shiver runs up my spine. I had not suspected the plots that Elwah clearly had foreseen would take place. Saeed looks at me, a look of unease on his face.

Aïschah breaks the silence. "Now you know what Elwah is most concerned about. Azizi, Saeed, do you understand the potential danger you are in and the threat you represent, having taken possession of a Sacred Sapphire each?"

A heavy silence weighs upon us all.

Faruq clears his throat to gain attention. "Mahjira, I am a soldier. I have seen the power that Azizi commands. It is fearsome. The legend of the Sapphires that I know, states that even if one of them were to be at the head of an army, that would be sufficient to instil fear in the enemy. The power that each of them holds would be enough to fill anyone with dread; even if it came to that, to utterly defeat any opponent. I do not understand then how it is that anyone on the Council or other, would seek or even dare to harm them?"

Aïschah smiles knowingly, glances at Sahir and addressing Faruq, gently states, "General Faruq, truly spoken as a soldier, and I mean no disrespect. When Azizi went in search of the Tear of Apphat and ultimately sought to rescue Prince Shahulm, he surrounded himself with soldiers." She allows a moment for that concept to sink in. "The power of the Sacred Sapphires is not meant for destruction or defeat, they are the Tears of the Cosmos, they are meant to inspire peace. That is why as you say, the legend states that a Sapphire at the head of an army would easily defeat its enemy; not by destroying them, but by suppressing their need for violent conflict and restore a harmony between people." Faruq blushes a little finally understanding. "You see, no matter how powerful Azizi's magic was or is, he is forbidden to use it to harm any individual. If he did, even in a momentary loss of his emotions, the power would immediately turn against him and destroy him. That is exactly what happened to the sorceress."

His cheeks blushing still, Faruq nods in acceptance. "Thank you Mahjira. I do understand now. As soldiers we become responsible for the protection of those who ultimately will restore the peace and harmony in the world."

"Well-spoken General Faruq." She pauses a moment, her mind seeking something else she adds, "the legend has often been misinterpreted. Those that seek power and only power at all costs, believe that the Sacred Sapphires will give them the authority to rule the world. They are fooling themselves. Yes, the Sapphires do increase the magic ability of the one who holds them, but his or her intent must be pure – the power is meant to be used for the benefit of all, not for an individual to gratify himself."

Aïschah turns to Sahir who endorses, "I agree with everything Aïschah has said." Turning to Saeed with the love a parent would have for his child, Sahir asks, "Do you understand everything that has been said, Saeed?"

Saeed briefly looks at me and turning back to Sahir, "Yes Mahjir. I do."

Sahir is about to say something else, stops himself mid thought, shakes his head once and looks across to Aïschah, who tilts her head slightly in an inquiring fashion. He immediately responds with a shake of his head. The exchange was too quick for me to perceive any information. Aïschah turns back to Faruq.

"General Faruq, the instruction from Elwah is clear. You will need to take Azizi and Saeed away from Naasée. You will need to do so without leaving any possible trace of your passage or destination. They are to remain hidden and under your protection until such time as Master Sahir and I call for them." Turning to me and Saeed, "Azizi and Saeed, we advise you both to limit your use of magic to the most essential needs. And even then, you are advised not to perform any act of magic that could leave enough of a trace of power that would immediately lead someone sensitive to magic to either of you."

We both answer, "Yes, godmother." "Yes, Mahjira."

There is an abrupt tremor. A deafening roar resonates through the cavern as an avalanche of rocks suddenly crash down and blocks the entrance to the cave.

Faruq and the twins, Rauf and Isamadeen rush to the entrance, short swords drawn and ready, only to step back and turn with a look of defeat.

"The rocks have completely sealed the entrance and the roof on this side looks as though it could collapse any moment." Faruq's voice is solemn. "Mahjira, is there another way out of the cave?"

"I do not know of any."

"It seems our presence has been discovered." Sahir looks at my godmother, "do you think that the farstep using the power of the sapphires revealed our movements?"

"I think you're right, but then why this simple act of sabotage? Knowing that we linked with the power of the sapphires, surely whoever contrived this simple plot must have realised that we have others here and that we cannot use Farstep with untrained individuals." Her voice pointedly identifies Faruq, Isamadeen and Rauf. "For you and me to use our powers now to remove the blockage, will be to reveal our presence and our goal to hide and protect Saeed and Azizi."

"I agree." Sahir's voice and expression carry a hint of frustrated defeat. "It seems that the objective is to keep us prisoners here."

"Azizi?" I turn to Faruq. "I do not know who caused this or who is on the other side. Whoever it is they can't possibly be friendly."

I nod in agreement, not sure what he is trying to say.

"Azizi, I have witnessed what you can do with an avalanche of rocks that once blocked our way." I stare at Faruq, slowly remembering the mad man in the Huda Pass.

"I think that it is too late for your godmother or Master Sahir not to reveal their presence or their intention to protect you. Whoever thought of this scheme, must suspect that you are all in here." I acknowledge for him to go on. "They may simply hope to isolate you and keep you here until they devise another plan to capture you." He takes a moment, swallows hard before continuing. "I remember the magic that you used in the Huda pass. You were able to utterly reduce the rubble of rocks to dust and in no way did your act cause harm. Even the madman who was standing atop the mound of rocks simply collapsed into confusion and hysteria."

"Faruq, are you asking me to do the same here?"

His piercing blue eyes hold mine for a moment, he then turns to Aïschah and Sahir. "Is that not a possibility? Once the rocks removed, my soldiers and I will simply charge forward with Azizi and Saeed between us, and we will make a swift exit into the desert. Our horses are not far from here and well hidden."

Aïschah and Sahir exchange looks. "I agree with general Faruq. It is too late to conceal the fact that we took the boys away and are attempting to protect them from the Council. I do not know who it is that has instigated this," she briefly gestures to the front of the cave, "and who they have convinced to join forces with them. It is possible that only one or two individuals are responsible. On the other hand, Prince Elwah may be losing his authority on the council if the Elders have allowed this."

Sahir nods in agreement, "Then we cannot allow them to simply take us. Aïschah, you know the spell they will use against us if they gain entry. Either way, we cannot surrender or wait for them to take us."

My godmother looks absorbed, the serious look she has when considering a difficult problem. She takes a deep breath and lets it out slowly.

"Godmother?" Aïschah meets my eyes. "Godmother, what spell is Master Sahir speaking about?"

She sighs once more. "It is an ancient and rarely used spell. It is used only in case a magician has somehow lost their grasp on reality. It is a spell that binds the magician and prevents them for a time, from using their magic. Essentially it renders the individual submissive. It is called the Binding Spell."

A cold shiver runs through me. I had never considered that the Magicians of this land would ever conceive such a spell to capture one of their own.

Aïschah suddenly stands, takes a few paces before turning back to us. "It is frustrating not to know what is taking place in Naasée at the moment." Her facial features harden, coming to a decision, she looks directly at me. "Azizi, you are close to Elwah, do you think it would be possible for you to create a mind link with him and see through his eyes what is happening?"

Silence fills the cave, broken only by the soft echo of a few pebbles still falling at the front entrance.

My stomach tightens. The eyes of everyone in the cave are upon me, the expectation weighs on my shoulders. *You have been chosen for this...* the voice I heard in the cave of the calling resonates in my head. "Yes, godmother I know I can. It would be as easy as calling you when I was still learning."

The tension in the cave eases.

"Good! Mahjir Sahir and I will then attempt to link with your mind. That way our presence will not be detected."

An unsettling memory of the sorceress as she manipulated my dream, surfaces from the part of me that still lurks in darkness. *What if I am caught and unable to withdraw and become trapped?*

"Saeed will help you, Azizi." With uncanny accuracy my godmother has read my thoughts and understood the doubt.

Saeed looks at her then me, a question in his eyes.

"Saeed, Azizi will go into a light trance and will attempt to reach Elwah's mind to find out what is happening in Naasée. If something were to go wrong and someone found out what he was doing, it is possible that they would attempt to trap him in his mind. If that occurs, listen closely to Azizi's mind. If he calls for help, all you need to do is focus on your heart and in your mind simply pull Azizi back here—in his body. All you need to do is hold his hand and relax."

Without question and with absolute trust, Saeed sits next to me and immediately takes my right hand in his. My godmother looks on tenderly at the devotion Saeed displays.

I take a few deep breaths and visualise the light of the Stone of Elwah, its essence being within me, the light shines behind my closed eyes lids with an intensity that is almost blinding. In my mind, softly I call out, "Elwah, Elwah?"

I have barely uttered his name a second time and the magical blue eyes I beheld as a young boy in my godmother's fireplace, stare back at me. His voice loaded with anxiety speaks to my mind, "Azizi, are you safe?"

"We are safe, but we are trapped. Someone has caused an avalanche of rocks at the mouth of the Cave of Gibrar. My godmother is anxious to know what is happening in Naasée."

"This is very dangerous Azizi. Is Aïschah protecting the communication between us? I do not want someone here to trace your thoughts."

"Elwah, I am sure she is doing just that. Do you know who caused this trap?"

"All the Elders are here. No one is missing. Azizi, you don't have much time, listen carefully." Elwah momentarily breaks our link but not before I overhear an authoritative voice call out to him that he is required in the Council chamber. With considerable effort

on my part to maintain the link, I follow Elwah as he makes his way to the Council Chamber.

Elwah's voice suddenly stern in my head instructs, "*Tell Aïschah that it is now imperative she understands Saeed's birth chart. For now, just watch and listen and do not attempt to speak directly to me.*"

All the Elders are assembled. The Chamber looks even more oppressive at night with just a few wall torches lit. Some of the Elders have raised elf lights, adding to the gloomy shadows of the Council Chamber.

Some Elders are whispering to each other, others are exchanging anxious glances. Master Sindarin is quietly contemplative. The places where my godmother and master Sahir would sit, are pointedly vacant, leaving only eight elders including Elwah.

By the time Elwah walks in, Master Ahmad is already standing, a look of malicious intent written all over his face. Elwah calmly takes his usual place, scans the room making deliberate eye contact with every individual present. Some look away, others attempt to smile and give a small bow in his direction. The occasional whispers create a current, making the air ripple with tension.

"Where are the bearers of the Sacred Tears of Apphat?" Ahmad's accusatory tone cuts through the chamber, bringing the congregation to an uneasy silence.

"Hmm." Elwah stands and responds, "I am a little confused. Members of the Council, I do not remember calling for an urgent meeting at this hour." A few Elders turn to stare at Ahmad. "The bearers of the Sacred Tears, Master Ahmad, are probably resting following their ordeal. And to alleviate your obvious concern, I am certain that they are in a safe place, away from possible harm or abduction."

The last word sends a ripple through the assembly, the reference to his own abduction, raised only a few dahé ago, stings a few consciences.

"And where have you taken them? You have no right to take them under your control."

Elwah allows himself a small sarcastic smile, "I can assure you Master Ahmad, that if I had taken them anywhere, I would now be with them to protect them with all my power." Ahmad is about to say something else, Elwah cuts him off with a raised hand, "Needless to say, as I have just done, that they are safe. Where that is, even I am unable to give you that information."

"Master Elwah," Master Elim, who performed the ritual of opening the gateway, stands up, addressing Elwah, "I do not question the need to protect the bearers of the Sacred Tears. It is obvious by their absence in this chamber, that Mahjira Aïschah and Master Sahir have taken the boys away. Do you doubt the Council would keep them safe?"

Elwah allows the silence to grow as he glares at the assembled Elders. "May I remind each and every one of you, that it was not so long ago, that this Council sat on their learned hands, while the forces of evil manipulated some if not several members of THIS COUNCIL!" Elwah suddenly raises his voice on the last two words, sending a shudder amongst them, "that this council did nothing to prevent my capture." Like a sheet of ice, ready to crack, silence hangs over the assembly; so palpable that even I, who is not standing in that chamber, tremble as a cold shiver runs up my spine.

"Master Elim, you have asked me, and by inclusion, you have asked all those here present, if I doubt that the Council could keep the Bearers of the Sacred Tears Safe? Let me ask all of you a question," Elwah pauses seeming to gather his thoughts, then turning his eyes, which have suddenly taken on the blue of the power of his magic, directly on Ahmad. "When the stones were made manifest, and the boys were given a command by the Sacred Twins to Choose, please, masters, take your time to consider this, whose voice was it that instructed Saeed, and what advice was he given?"

All eyes have now turned to Ahmad whose face has paled. Some Elders shaking their heads in embarrassment.

Ahmad is on his feet, almost shouting. "It was his right to choose both! Only one Master should be holding both as was mandated to King Apphat by the Goddess herself. It would have been his duty then, to surrender both for safekeeping with one of the masters of the Council of Elders." Pausing only for a breath, he shouts again, "It is outrageous, absolutely unheard of, that such a responsibility and authority should have been given to two inexperienced young magician, one with the most basic of training in performing simple tricks."

The Council appears to be divided. With the physical response to the last statement, it is obvious that doubt has infiltrated some minds about the suitability of Azizi and Saeed.

"So, Master Ahmad, you then question the wisdom of the goddess Ishtar and the Sacred twins in making that decision?"

The whispers suddenly hush and an uncomfortable silence returns. No one in their right mind would dare the blasphemy of questioning the goddess' wisdom.

"Master Elwah?" the genteel tones of Mahjira Mitra breaks the silence.

"Mahjira, what is your question?"

"I do not question the goddess. With my ability to summon Ancient Guardians, I can vouchsafe that it is not an easy task and is riddled with risks for the summoner. I acknowledge that both young magicians, as untrained as Ahmad claims, nevertheless performed the act of summoning their personal Guardians with exceptional ease." Elwah urges her on with a knowing smile. "But it remains to know why two were chosen and why these two specifically."

"Mahjira Mitra, it is the question that has bested the greatest minds since the Sacred Sapphires were given to King Apphat. I will ask for Master Sindarin to verify and support my claim." A brief look at Sindarin gains his approval with a nod.

"First and foremost, unknown to most magicians and learned masters, there are several prophesies and sacred verses that have been written on the subject, most by King Apphat himself. Most of us only know of the final warning the great sage gave to his followers. I assume that I do not have to repeat that?" Mahjira shakes her head a note of embarrassment flushes her features. "Mahjira, would you like to know the spell that young Azizi pronounced as he defeated the sorceress?" Elwah waits for a significant moment, Mitra's face flushes a little and the rest of the assembly waits upon Elwah's words.

"He used a simple spell that was contained in one of the Sacred Parvus of King Apphat, with all his integrity intact and a pure heart, Azizi pronounced the following words: '*Water and Salt that maketh the Tears of Joy and Sorrow cannot be one without the other. Pain and sweetness go hand in hand, I release you!*'

The power in those words still send a shudder up my spine;

a silence like a storm cloud heavy with rain, descends upon the assembly.

"The meaning, Mahjira Mitra, as Azizi intuitively understood, is that the Sacred Sapphires cannot be held by one individual without destroying that individual." He pauses a moment, looking for Ahmad's reaction to this new knowledge. "I cannot reveal the rest of that Parvus, it is not appropriate at this point to allow that knowledge." Ahmad begins to fidget; the knowledge bothers him and thwarts his desire to hold both Sapphires.

"You will agree with me though, that given what Master Ahmad would describe as 'basic training', Azizi demonstrated a knowledge and power well beyond most of the abilities of those currently present." The insult does not go unnoticed. Many heads hang in shame, some are obviously offended by the words but would not dare to argue, unless their lack of knowledge was to prove their inability.

"So now Mahjira Mitra, let me address your other question: that of 'why those two?'"

Again, several members wait upon Elwah's words.

"It's very simple and yet complex. Allow me a moment to gather my thoughts." Elwah suddenly makes a gesture with one hand behind his back, which I understand is a subtle protection against mind interference. With his other hand against the side of his head, his voice suddenly clearly resonates in my head, "*Azizi, has Aïschah examined Saeed's birth chart?*"

I turn to my godmother, who has been in deep conversation with Master Sahir. The knowledge he conveyed using his mind slowly seems to have deeply affected her. First, she nods in acknowledgement, then her eyes widen and when given the final pieces of information, her face pales as she stares at Saeed and then me. Eventually coming to the same conclusion as Sahir.

"I think so Elwah. She appears to have understood something and agrees with it."

"Good, I will call her if I need her. For now, continue to watch and be silent."

"Mahjira, I hope you would agree with me that the goddess Ishtar would have easily rejected anyone who she deemed not worthy to receive the Sacred Tears?" Mitra nods. "Simple question now." Mahjira Mitra appears nervous. "Without going too much into esoteric matters or ancient texts, Mahjira who or what represents the Sacred Tears of Apphat?"

Mitra is about to blurt out something, bites her lower lip blushing at the obvious answer, she whispers, "The Sacred Twins."

"Correct. So now you know that the Sacred Tears cannot be held by one, but in fact are meant to be held by two individuals who, if the power is called upon, must not be separated. Does this not imply that whoever holds the Sacred Sapphires must also be twins?"

The revelation seems to have confounded and astonished the Elders into absolute silence.

My jaw hangs loose. I turn and stare at Saeed and then at my godmother whose expression of astonishment has not diminished in the slightest.

"But master Elwah," the master of visions, Master Vasilis half raises himself in his seat, "those boys are not twins."

A soft chuckle is heard, heads turn, and watch Master Sindarin suppress a laugh with his hand.

"As I said it is both simple and complex. The stars have aligned for the first time in one hundred years for this event. Mahjira

Mitra, Azizi and Saeed are twin Souls."

Only the distant thunder of a wave crashing at the base of Naasée can be heard.

A bolt of lightning going through my body would have had the same impact as these words. I turn and stare at Saeed, who having seen and heard everything so far stares back at me, first with a look of shock that is quickly replaced with a smile of such awe and love that my heart suddenly beats like a drum.

He releases my hand and reaching out, wraps his arms around me, holds me in the softest embrace I have only known once in my life.

My godmother is looking at us both, shaking her head in mild disbelief and smiling her most loving smile.

CHAPTER THREE

"That is preposterous!" Master Ahmad has not given up his fight. "How could you even know that?"

All eyes turn from Ahmad to Elwah and back again.

"By comparing both Star Charts drawn at their birth. I was able to draw that conclusion, which was verified by both Master Sahir of the Huda People and Mahjira Aïschah, whose reputation as an interpreter of Star charts is, in my opinion, equal to none."

A malicious smile stretches across Master Ahmad's lips, with a glint in his eyes, "It would be favourable, of course, to have both of them confirm this, your Excellency." The last words dripping with sarcasm.

Without blinking, Elwah bows slightly before answering in a suave tone of voice edged with steely intent, "Master Ahmad, could I indulge your generosity and request that you send your servant Tabrass to fetch the masters? Would you please call him so that we can all hear your instructions?"

The master suddenly pales.

"And while he is here, I would really be interested to hear about the gift of oil you had your servant Tabrass deliver to Saeed, and the reason for doing so." Elwah mockingly feigns a memory loss, "If I recall, the one that was distilled from orange blossoms." Elwah says nothing for the shortest pause before adding, "or perhaps it was distilled from something else, Master Ahmad?"

A short silence follows while everyone waits on Master Ahmad's reply.

"Master Elwah, you seem to be inferring something important. I think for clarity I would appreciate a detailed explanation." Master Ngaway, master of spells and incantations firm but gentle voice cuts above the whispers.

"It was just a gift! An apology for the fact my manservant had mishandled him." Ahmad's voice is trembling with rage which he is desperately trying to disguise as indignation.

"Master Ahmad, you surprise me. I have never known you to gift something without an expectation of a favour in return." The tension in the room is electric.

Elwah scans the assembly, before addressing Ahmad, "Master Ahmad, I can confirm for you, since you are reluctant to speak about it, that though the oil was distilled from orange blossoms, which happen to be Saeed's favourite scent, was however, also laced with something else. That additional ingredient is subtle yet powerful enough to render the user pliable if not completely obedient."

Elwah raises his hand interrupting Ahmad's interjection, "Master Ahmad, please do not insult my intelligence. Two other magicians were able to detect the added substance. So, since Sahir, master of potions is not here, let me ask Master Ngaway as master of spells and incantation the following. Master Ngaway if I were to infuse merely a few drops of Omao in a small vial of distilled orange blossoms, how would that affect the end fragrance?"

Ngaway focusses a moment. "The dominant fragrance of Omao is sandalwood and also has a bitter after note." His brow creases as he applies his sense of imagination to the end fragrance, "the sandalwood would blend fairly well with the orange blossom lending a deeper, warm note to the sweetness of the orange; the bitter note would also complement the orange, giving it a realistic fragrance of orange that has matured. Overall making the Omao almost undetectable."

Ahmad has gone silent.

"And what effect would such a combination of fragrance have on the wearer?"

Ngaway pauses, swallows nervously before answering, "If worn regularly over a period of time, it would render the wearer susceptible to impressions and also vulnerable to the Vox Imperii and binding spells." An uncomfortable silence follows, eyes stare at Master Ahmad are then quickly averted.

"Is this your assertion, master Elwah?" Ngaway asks to fill the silence, obviously uncomfortable.

Elwah's face, a cold mask, devoid of emotion stares directly at Master Ahmad.

"Yes, Master Ngaway. It is."

"Can this be verified?"

"Once Saeed and Master Sahir are here, it will be without doubt. The effect of the oil is still detectable on Saeed himself and I understand he still has the vial of oil in his possession."

“How was he able to resist it then, at such a young age?” Mahjira Mitra’s gentle tones cut through the tension.

“Hmm. Although I had detected the subtle fragrance early, I was curious to see how far Master Ahmad would take this action. It is fortunate that Young Azizi is an adept at potions having been trained by his godmother, a leading herbalist and potion maker. He also has a refined sense of smell. He is exceptionally talented at creating talismans. In this case, once detected and with Saeed’s approval, Azizi designed a powerful talisman of protection that would not interfere with Saeed’s other abilities.”

An astonished murmur of admiration with expression of “such talent at a young age, amazing” sweeps through the assembly.

“Master Ahmad, your intent on making Saeed obedient and the prompting for him to acquire both Sacred Sapphires, leaves me with unanswered questions. It remains for you to explain yourself and if you can, clarify your intentions.”

Nods of agreement follows, and everyone waits on Ahmad’s response.

Slowly and with great care, Ahmad stands. His face is pale, his tense jaw gives him a gaunt and tired look.

“I have always maintained that the Sacred Tears of Apphat, if they were to be recalled, should be given into the hands of trained and experienced Master Magicians.”

Some of the Elders nod slowly, obviously agree. Small creaks from the chairs and platform break the hushed silence.

“Since you were determined to appoint these young men to receive the Sacred Tears, then it is necessary that they should answer to the Council of Elders and be placed in the care of experienced Elders.”

"Mmm. I see. First of all, Master Ahmad, I did not appoint Azizi and Saeed. They were selected a long time ago by the goddess. Their role was revealed in countless prophesies, including several parvii verses written by Apphat the Wise, himself. Master Sindarin knows the prophesies and parvii I refer to." All eyes look at master Sindarin who smiling benevolently, nods in agreement.

"More disturbingly, Master Ahmad, is your intention to have them under the 'control' of the Council of Elders. Do you propose to hold them prisoners here until the Sapphires are required? Would they then never be free to grow into adulthood, to have their own life? You want them to be at your beck and call; to be subjugated to your will and the will of these magicians? You would use them any way you see fit? And then, Master Ahmad, when they no longer fit your purpose, would you just dispose of them—in the same manner you decided to dispose of me? I do not think that this was ever the intention of Ishtar!"

A sticky silence weighs upon the assembly. More than a few Elders have bowed their heads in apparent shame.

"In any case, your excellency," Ahmad's voice is dripping with contempt, "since you no longer hold the Sacred Stone of Elwah, it is fitting that you relinquish your title of Haafiz. In fact, I think that your title as Prince of Naasée is unsustainable."

Elwah deliberately raises a hand to his forehead smiling all the while. His command in my mind is dispassionate: "*Now*!"

The doors to the Chamber suddenly burst open. Hasan marches in, dressed in full official uniform as captain of the Royal Guards. Half a dozen royal guards in full armour, follow and take their place around the chamber.

"What is the meaning of this?" Ahmad's face is red with anger.

With all the unyielding voice of a commanding general, Hasan challenges the assembly: "As Captain of the Royals Guards and personal attendant to His Highness Lord Elwah, Custodian and Prince of Naasée, it is my duty and role as his bodyguard to protect him from all harm, either real or perceived." Hasan draws his sword.

The shock creates a brief silence. Some of the Elders have stood up, others are still seated in disbelief.

"The meaning? Master Ahmad? It has been obvious, at least to me, that your intent has always been a take-over. To place yourself at the head of this Council. To control and wield the power of the Sacred Tears for your own ends."

The shocked whispered exchanges quieten down as Elwah raises his hand for silence.

"Mahjirs, Mahjiras, I agree–the appointment of the Haafiz and title of prince of Naasée, based solely on physical attributes as proof of the reincarnation of the previous ruler, is no longer sensible. This custom should come to an end." Elwah pauses long enough for the Elders to hang on his words.

"What matters most is that the Sacred Sapphires have been recalled and are once again in the world. I advise very strongly against any idea to appoint the boys in any capacity on this Council; or for either of them to be subjugated to the will of anyone of this Council. For my own, I am happy to resign my title and to leave this place and live a life of rest away from this political turmoil." A wave of shocked exclamations sweeps the assembly. Most are opposed to such an idea. Elwah's face changes slightly as an amused smile floats across his lips. "In fact, I also propose as such that this Council be dissolved." The stunned silence that follows is brief. The voice of Master Suffrah is heard above the clamour, "Master

Elwah, this cannot be! Who will administer the City of Naasée and its people?"

In the short silence that follows, Elwah calmly replies, "Master Suffrah, I see that none of the Elders here are willing to stand for me, except for my trusted personal guard." Elwah chuckles softly to himself. "Masters, Hasan has administered this town and its people since he took office four scores ago. I am certain that it will continue to flourish under his care and administration."

Elwah deliberately steps down from the platform, he turns to take in the entire chamber, releases a long sigh, speaking more to himself, "I take my leave, I release this position and all its burdens. I take my magic with me to live a fruitful and joyful life. Hasan, would you see me safely out of this den of wolves?"

Hasan steps next to his prince, sword still drawn and escorts Elwah out of the chamber. Briefly, as the link begins to lose clarity, Elwah stumbles slightly, catches Hasan's arm and with his head held up, walks out of the chamber. Only their receding steps can be heard in the silence at their backs.

The link is broken, and I am back in the cave of Gibrar. My godmother's eyes are filled with tears. Master Sahir sits frozen in place, his face pale, his brow knitted. Faruq, Isamadeen and Rauf stand with their heads bowed. My heart sinks a little, my gut feels cold at the decisions Elwah has just taken.

Saeed is still next to me, recognising my sense of confusion and shock, simply continues to hold my hand.

"It is now imperative for us to leave this place. Elwah will be safe with Hasan." Cutting through the cold air of the cave, my godmother's quiet voice holds a mixture of firm resolve. Aïschah turns to me, "Azizi, can you clear the entrance to the cave?" It's a request, her eyes hold no doubt.

I nod and move towards the entrance, her words of training echoing in my head, *always ask your Source.* I go within and bow, it requires no time at all for the feeling of assurance that permission is granted.

Focussing on my source, taking a deep breath I raise the power from within. A strong current climbs up my spine, reaching my heart. A burst of flames fills my head, my eyes water, tears stream down my face, and I taste salt on my lips. My entire being is suddenly filled with energy, which glows the purest blue. It fills me, surrounds me, power flows through me like I have never experienced before. There is no need for me to raise my hands, there is no need for me to command, with a mere thought, the energy surges forward from me and with no more than a hiss, the avalanche of rocks crumbles to dust. A strong gust of fresh air from the desert fills the cave.

The power recedes, I am left staring at the night sky, stars glittering over the adjoining sand dunes and above the distant city walls of Naasée. My body is energised, my skin tingles, there is none of the nausea or tiredness that plagued me during my training. I feel exhilarated, my back is straight, my chest expands, my shoulders are free of any burden, a sensation of floating fills me, I feel powerful. Saeed's hand slips into mine and gently squeezes it. I squeeze it back, turning to him with a smile, knowing that whatever power still blazes in my eyes, he at least will not recoil from me. His emerald green eyes smile back.

Faruq is the first behind me, followed by Isamadeen and Rauf.

"Quickly, follow us!" He commands. With drawn swords, they step casually to the entrance, my god mother and Sahir follow closely.

My feet casually step through and stir the fine sand that moments ago were solid rocks. A part of me is fascinated at the power that can do this.

As we approach the mouth of the cave, I can hear the soft wailing of a man. Stepping out, we are confronted with a man bent over on the sand, holding his arm. His arm is visibly burnt, and his hand bent at an unnatural angle. I recognise Tabrass, Master Ahmad's servant, sobbing with pain.

Tabrass, only a few steps away, looks up. "I am sorry, the master ordered me to! Please don't kill me." His whole demeanour and voice now sound pathetic. Gone is his previous arrogance. I understand now, why Ahmad blanched at Elwah's request to send for his servant.

My godmother steps forward, looks on pitifully at the man kneeling before us. A spark of her compassion as a healer briefly flashes in her eyes, she addresses him directly in a stern voice, "Your master ordered you to do this, but did your master also teach you the spell to bring down these rocks, or is that your own doing?"

Tabrass nods his head, "I have no training. He told me it would be safe."

Aïschah's voice is suddenly cold. "It seems you have paid for your act of foolishness Tabrass. The spell has rebounded on you. Leave this place and leave your master, he is not worth serving." Aïschah deliberately walks away, leaving the servant sobbing on the sand.

Rauf and Isamadeen briefly look down with pity before stepping away.

I hesitate, something in me wants to forgive and offer healing. Saeed still holds my hand, leans in and whispers, "Azizi, I know. This is not your doing Azizi, let him seek healing with someone else."

Looking into Saeed's eyes, I see no hatred or condemnation of the man who tried to trick him. I nod in agreement, compassion still whispering in my heart, I turn to face the man who had simply followed orders of a selfish individual. I turn to Ahmad's servant meeting his fearful eyes, "Tabrass, go to the foothills of the Asfaine mountains, there you will find someone who can heal your arm. Take my godmother's advice, leave this place and do not come back."

I pull on Saeed's hand and lead him away, catching up to Faruq who has been patiently waiting. His piercing blue eyes penetrating my inner being, he acknowledges my kindness adding, "I speak only as a soldier Azizi, in my view it would have been kinder to dispatch him here and now."

The thought makes me shiver. A soldier's spirit must be strong to make life or death decisions so quickly and effectively.

I acknowledge his comment and follow his lead into the desert. It's not long before I catch sight of a low outcrop of rocks and shrubs outlined against the starlit sky, and the silhouettes of horses tethered.

We reach the outcrop; Faruq and his companions had wrapped pieces of material around the horses' bits so that they would not clink and attract unwanted attention.

As we come up onto the horses I stop in my tracks, a knot around my heart. I count five horses. I realise then that Aïschah and Sahir will not be able to escape with us. Confused as to the plan, I turn to my godmother and Sahir.

"Godmother, what was your plan?"

"Azizi, the plan was simple. To see you and Saeed safe with Faruq and his soldiers and make sure of your escape as quickly as possible."

"What about you and master Sahir? What will you do? What if the Elders come looking for you and use their binding spell?" My voice is shaking, sounding desperate.

"Azizi, your safety and Saeed's are more important right now than anything else."

No! my mind refuses to accept that they be left behind. I desperately search my mind for a solution. Using my godmother's technique for calming the mind, I focus on visualising a solution where both are safe. Staring up at the sky to better centre myself, my attention is drawn to a star blinking in the night sky. It is part of the Fire Beast constellation, it blinks orange. A clear image forms of a narrow treacherous passage burning red in the late sunlight.

"Saeed?" I call out, only realising that he is next to me.

"Azizi?" he whispers back.

"Saeed, do you think that my godmother would be welcomed and protected with your tribe in the Huda Pass?"

"Yes Azizi, they can farstep to the Huda. Master Sahir is the Mage of the Huda People, he will know the way. My mother's tribe will look after them."

I let out a sigh of relief. I look at my godmother. She heard the exchange and slowly nods in agreement. Saeed turns to her, "Mahjira Aïschah, our mage, Master Sahir will explain everything to our leader Gaisha. I am sure she will understand and offer the protection of her people. The Huda Pass is well protected; no one can enter it without permission."

I am about to turn toward the horses when I see shadows approach at a deliberate walking pace. I freeze. The night light is behind them, their faces are obscured by deep hoods over their heads. My heart skips a beat as I recognise the gait of one of them. Hasan steps forward and briefly holds me in his arms, Elwah is with him.

Turning to Elwah, "Did you have to take such drastic a step as to resign?" I ask him.

Elwah's face as enigmatic as ever, smiles a small sad grin. "It was necessary Azizi. Nothing else would have brought an end to the endless arguments." Turning slightly to my godmother he continues, "rest assured, the elders will soon realise Ahmad's ambition. Chaos will reign for a while. The Elders will eventually realise that none of them have contributed to the wise and safe administration of Naasée and that some of them are here only to serve their self-interest. They will eventually understand the need for strong and wise leadership. I hope that they will not be tempted to seek either of you to use your powers to restore order. The Sapphires can only be used to restore harmony – but only if those seeking it are willing to submit themselves to the proper order of things. That will require wisdom and patience on their part."

A small sadness modulates his voice as he adds, "Also – any insistence on retaining any title or power, would make me vulnerable to future attack. This way, even if they are not entirely convinced that I have relinquished my titles willingly, they will leave me alone – their focus will now centre on the obvious power void." Elwah takes a deep breath, releasing it slowly, "You and Saeed have made it out safely. Now Azizi, do not look back and do not delay, go with Faruq." Elwah's voice is now stern.

Elwah turns to Hasan resting his hand casually on his arm. Hasan looks at me lovingly, nods his head to Elwah whose eyes take on a brilliant sapphire blue, and they both vanish before our eyes.

Aïschah briefly converses with Sahir, turns to me. "Azizi, heed Elwah's advice. Do not delay."

Sahir steps forward to Saeed, lovingly extends a hand to him and gently caresses his face. "Saeed, when I see you next, I will tell you of your father and your heritage." Saeed is left gaping, not sure how to respond, he blushes and nods his head.

Sahir and Aïschah stand together as Saeed and I mount our respective horse. Faruq and the twins are already waiting, their mounts impatiently pawing the ground. We turn the horse's head to follow Faruq as he leads us out into the desert. My mount already pacing out into a gentle trot, I look back. My heart sinks, a shadow has stepped over one of the dunes and I distinctly hear an angry voice call out, "Dybbuk!" The sound alone sends shivers up my spine. I see Aïschah stagger. She makes a vague gesture to ward off the spell. She stumbles forward as Sahir catches her. I hear her thoughts, urgent and firm, *Azizi do not engage! Reserve your power for good!* While holding her, Sahir initiates the farstep and they both disappear.

Anger rises in me, tears suddenly flood my eyes, I sense her mind burning with agony. My horse following the lead of the others has broken into a full gallop. A part of me is screaming for revenge. I recognised the voice – it was unequivocally, Ahmad's voice, tinted with power and greed.

Desperate, I reach out again to my godmother, my head is suddenly filled with a burning pain, and then nothing, as if a light has gone out. A single frustrating thought emerges, *off guard; not quick enough to repel.* A rational part of my mind recognises it for what it is: *this is the result of a binding spell.*

The shadow of Faruq's mount lengthens on the sand and breaks into a resolute gallop. Sensing the urgency, all our mounts follow. Unprepared for the sudden movement, I lean low on my horse's neck and hold on to the reins.

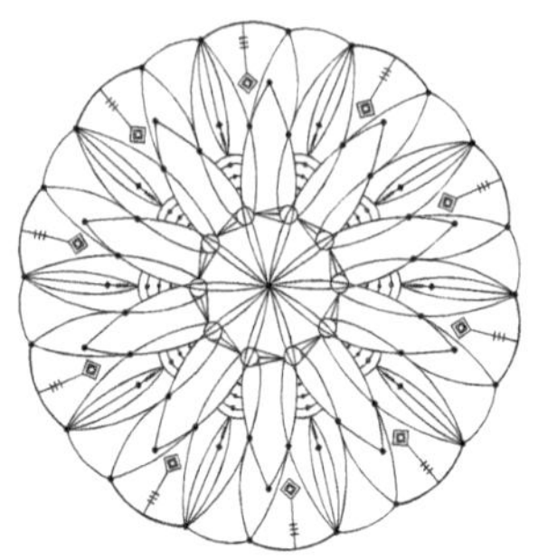

CHAPTER FOUR

Like a bejewelled cool blue drape, the colour of the shemagh of the Tassili people, the Great Desert of Keyab engulfs us with its starlit sky,

Tears are still coursing down my face, the rushing cold night air whipping them away. A cold rage fills my stomach like a heavy stone. My rational mind argues with my fear, attempting to convince me that my godmother is fine; she is an experienced seeress and healer.

Faruq is relentless in his speed. Just as I think my body can take no more of the unending rhythm of the horse and the pain in my legs, Faruq holds one hand up and slows down to a trot. Allowing the horses to cool down first before calling a complete stop.

In my attempt to dismount my horse, my knees yield; I fall staggering to the ground and beat the sand with my fists, I give way to sobs of pure anger.

Saeed rushes to me, kneeling by my side, places a hand on my shoulders gently stroking my back, “I heard the curse Azizi.” he whispers, “Master Sahir is with her, he will look after her. I am sure your godmother will be fine.”

Half choking on my tears, I look at him, “I saw her stagger. I heard her say that she could not repel it, urging me to keep going. I felt her pain, Saeed!” I almost scream the last words out, uttering the words haltingly.

Saeed’s hand pauses, I see the worry in his eyes and a hint of uncertainty. I regret my outburst immediately, I draw a deep breath, “I am sorry Saeed. This is not your fault.”

“Have some water.” Faruq steps forward offering us both a flask. Settling first on his haunches, he sits cross legged facing me. “We are far from Naasée, we can rest a while here.” His piercing blue eyes, half shaded by his shemagh nevertheless look deeply into my being. I draw some strength from his calm composure and confidence.

“Azizi?” I realise that my focus has wandered. I shake my head. He looks at me, concern in his eyes. “We are heading to Ahvasar, the walled desert city.” He clarifies: “it’s a trading post and has a shipping port into the inlet of the ocean Malkizar. It is managed by one of the minor nobles but comes under the rule of my uncle the Sultan. We will take shelter there overnight.” He pauses a moment, “Will you be able to go on?” I nod my head, trying to remember if I have ever been to this town and draw a blank.

“Azizi, I have seen how magicians are able to vanish and travel to faraway places in the blink of an eye. I do not claim to understand this.” Faruq looks away for a short moment, then making up his mind, “Is it not possible for you and Saeed to do the same?”

I let a long breath out. “That technique is one learned much later in our training – well after the fifth initiation. I think I understand the principle, but I have never had it explained in detail. When Saeed and I appeared in the Cave of Gibrar, it was with the power of my godmother and master Sahir.” Faruq is pensive, I elaborate, “It is called ‘farstep’. Even if I were able to use that technique, there are some disadvantages to it. The magic leaves a trail of power that another trained magician can follow,” I gesture at the marks in the sand around us, “very much like footsteps in the sand.”

Faruq makes a deliberate counter gesture with his hand, erasing one of the marks. He looks at me questioningly. Smiling, I answer, “the power trail cannot be dealt with so easily. It is possible but requires much focus and much more knowledge than I have.”

Faruq, frowning nods his head in acknowledgement. He slowly stands up, stares a moment at the way we came, searching for any tell-tale signs of pursuit. “Drink as much water as you need, we will be able to refill these in Ahvasar.” He briefly looks up at the sky, “We should be able to make it just before dawn.” Looking down he adds “let me know when you and Saeed are ready to go on.” Faruq walks away and quietly chats to Isamadeen.

Saeed turns his head, looks briefly at me, and then stares at his hands.

“Azizi? Do you sense her?”

I turn to him, puzzled for a moment.

“Your godmother Azizi. Can you feel the power trail?”

An uncomfortable silence separates us.

“No Saeed, I can’t.” I take a quick breath and let it out slowly, desperate not to let my emotions take hold.

He places a hand on my shoulder again. A part of me wants to recoil; realising that this would hurt him, I hold still. A mixture of emotions like a small fire flickering in the centre of my being threatens to overflow; my hands make fists in anger, my stomach twists and clenches with a sense of futility and helplessness, my heart is pounding at the thought that my godmother may be hurt.

"Azizi?" Saeed's eyes are filled with concern.

I breathe out slowly through my nose, closing my lips tight, focussing my mind into the state Aïschah taught me in my early years; one that allows me to take control of my emotions.

"She raised me as her own child." Tears roll down my cheeks, my hands tighten into hard fists. Compassion fills Saeed's eyes as he silently stares at me.

"Saeed, I no longer feel the connection I have always had with her. I do not know where she is or how she is."

He nods and remains silent, knowing that words would never take away that pain.

"Azizi," he whispers. "I saw master Sahir take hold of her and initiate the farstep. I am sure that they are safe with my people in the Huda Pass." With a tinge of hope in his voice he adds, "Perhaps it is Master Sahir who hid the power trail for both of them?"

I am grateful for his attempt to quieten my mind. I force a smile and brush my tears away. "You are right Saeed. Thank you."

I slowly stand up, resolved to place my concerns aside, at least for now. A thought occurs to me, that we have left a visible trail upon the sand. It would require some power, but I could at least erase all evidence of our passage. This, at least is something I can do.

Saeed stands and begins to reach for his horse. "Come Saeed, you can help me with your power." He stares at me, I smile, "You see, I am still committed to your training into magic." The mixture of surprise and curiosity in his expression makes me smile. My heart is a little lighter, and I walk decisively to Faruq.

"Faruq." He turns, nods in response, his serious expression softening slightly.

"Azizi? You are ready to move out?"

"Yes, but not before I attend to our passage." He looks at me inquisitively. "Faruq, would you say that the prints we have left in the sand could easily lead a pursuer to us?"

He nods his head, not sure what I am saying. "Yes, Azizi. But there is little we can do about that now. I hope the morning wind may blow all traces away."

"Would it help if the wind were to rise a little earlier?"

The sudden look of awe and comprehension on Faruq's features, reminds me of the stare the companions gave when they witnessed my first act of magic in the Huda Pass.

"Azizi, I am not sure I fully understand. But yes, the earlier those marks on the sand are erased, the better to confuse anyone who may have already set out in pursuit."

I turn, Saeed is at my side with a look of amused curiosity and excitement on his face.

"Come Saeed, you and I will call the wind."

Isamadeen and Rauf who also overheard my exchange, follow with Faruq as Saeed and I take position at the crest of a dune, facing the way we came.

Saeed turns his head, waiting for instructions.

Leaning closely to him, I whisper, "I will tell you the name of the desert wind, Saeed. Not the mighty Cassim, but a smaller cousin and you and I will send it back to Naasée and erase all evidence of our passage."

He looks to me with a mixture of admiration and eagerness. "You already know part of its name." I smile at him as he tilts his head in inquiry. "Rih Habud." In answer to the crease in his brow, I explain, "Rih is for any wind, but when you say it together with Habud, it will form that small whirlwind that you have seen before."

He nods in response, "We will both call the wind. Since the wind is one of my elemental spirits, I could call it. But because the Habud is a guardian of the desert and not the mountains, I need your power combined with mine to manifest it."

"Azizi, how will we direct it to go back to Naasée?"

"You ask thoughtful questions Saeed." I briefly scan the way we have come. "The spirit of the wind needs to know the essence of the ones who left the footsteps on the sand. I will ask Faruq, Isamadeen and Rauf to gather a handful of sand and when I say so, to throw it into the air. The whirlwind will pick up the essence and much like an animal following the scent of its prey, it will follow the path we took and erase it at the same time."

Saeed absorbs that information and acknowledges the instruction.

"Saeed, this is a powerful spell. Much more complex than calling for light or a fire. It will require us both to use the power of the Sapphires. I will join hands with you and instruct you as we do it."

While Saeed contemplates what we are about to do, I turn to Faruq, Isamadeen and Rauf and explain what I require them to do. With wonder and a little curiosity, they gather a handful of sand and follow me to stand with Saeed.

I reach out and take Saeed's left hand, the one that represents his magical nature. He looks up, surprising me with a confident smile.

Speaking in soft voice, I begin my instruction: "Saeed, let your eyes wander over the sand. Now think of the times you have seen evidence of the wind blowing. The end of your shemagh as it flows when the wind picks it up. Think of the rustle of leaves of the nakhla, as the wind passes through them. Now remember how the desert air shimmers in the midday sun. Remember how it feels when you know that a cooling wind will soon appear."

Saeed's ability to drop into the centre of his being never ceases to amaze me. I turn to Faruq and the twins, "Be prepared."

"Now Saeed, focus you mind on your heart, speak to it with your mind and ask permission to use its power. A thrill of joy in your heart means that it is granted. With your mind let me know when you are ready."

I focus my own mind in the same way. The time it takes for a butterfly to take flight and I feel an almost overwhelming sense of joy fill me. I can feel Saeed's mind and even before he nods, I know that he is ready. With my mind I speak to his, *Together Saeed, we will speak the name of the wind and call it*. Both our voices mingle as we whisper: "RIH-HABUD -BETO!" emphasising each word.

The air appears to shimmer before us. The stars seem to blur as if a mist has covered the sky. I hear a whisper in the air, suddenly my shemagh blows away from my face. A small whirlwind no taller than knee high manifests in front of us. I turn to Faruq and the twins and nod. They stand there briefly in awe, and quickly throw their handful of sand toward the Habud. The air picks up the grains and gathers them into itself.

In my mind, I connect with Saeed and instruct him to utter out loud, the words that imbue it with the will to follow and erase out passage, "Rih Habud égétor peh!"

The whirlwind at once gathers speed and rises, now almost a man's height, it first makes a small circle. Finding the first signs of our passage, it suddenly moves off toward Naasée and the way we came. Growing in intensity and speed, picking up the sand wherever it travels, it races off toward the horizon. It takes no more than a few breaths for it to disappear out of sight.

I turn to face Faruq, "That should take care of any trace." He nods, astonishment still written over his face. Isamadeen looks on with deep respect. Rauf's face is a sculpture of awe and devotion; stepping forward he asks, "Saeed, is it permitted to touch your hand?"

Saeed, laughs innocently and holds out his hands. "They are just hands."

Rauf cautiously takes hold of his hands, a little choked with emotion, declares, "I swear to protect you with my life."

The lack of daylight cannot confirm whether Saeed's cheeks have turned the colour of sunset. He hesitates a moment not wanting to be rude, but obviously embarrassed at the devotion Rauf is displaying.

"Rauf, it was Azizi who made the magic happen, I just helped a bit."

I am charmed with the situation and deeply respectful of Saeed's humility, "We both did Saeed. Without you and the power of the Sacred Sapphire within, I could only do half the task."

"All of the Companions are sworn to defend both Azizi and Saeed." Faruq's pragmatic statement sobers up the situation and brings a small relief to the awkward moment.

CHAPTER FIVE

We resume our journey. I look up every now and again to the stars, gauging the direction we are heading. The constellation of the Fire Beast has risen slightly behind me to my right. It is almost mid sky. I conclude that we are travelling in a southerly direction. Directly south we would be on course for the city of Schiraz. I briefly wonder how far we are from the coastline of the ocean Elwah.

Some of the stars on the horizon ahead have faded, it will not be long before dawn. The steady rhythm of the horse's gait lulls me a little and loosens some of my thoughts. I steady my mind and focus on staying upright. My heart softens at the sight of Saeed just ahead of me, looking more like a young noble, one hand holding the bridle, the other loose by his side, sitting on his mount relaxed, moving gracefully with every stride the horse takes.

Sensing my gaze, he turns and beams a most glorious smile. I can't help but smile back; his eyes turn into the distance. I follow his gaze. Behind me, in the direction of the Asfaine mountains, the crescent moon of Camlac has just begun to appear over the horizon. It is a pale yellow. I shiver briefly at the memories of such an omen. A whisper of a breeze blows from the horizon, followed by a faint lamenting howl. My body suddenly tenses at the unmistakable sound of a lone wolf. I stare at Saeed, his head has turned forward again, he does not appear to have heard it.

I repeatedly turn my head, scanning the desert behind us. Doubts intrude my mind, perhaps it was the wind that caused the sound as it slipped between the dunes. A small heaviness weighs me down as I realise that we are approaching a city I do not remember ever visiting. I wonder what awaits us in this city, and whether the news and circumstances of our departure from Naasée has reached the ruling lord of the city.

The sky has begun to lighten to pale blue. Although the air is dry, it smells slightly of dust that has recently received rained. Even in the desert, morning dew settles on rare plants and the ground, giving off that familiar odour.

The vague irregular dark line on the horizon, takes shape. The outline of a wall with a few taller structures appears. The sun rising behind the city of Naasée, begins to light the desert, lengthening our shadows ahead of us and slightly to our right. Beams of sunlight catch some structures and glow a faint bronze. An elusive memory taunts me, I feel that I should be familiar with this city.

Sunlight strikes the city walls ahead of us, turning them into glistening ochre surfaces that have long been polished by the desert winds. A large closed wooden gate confronts us. Faruq stops his horse a short distance and waits. Rauf and Isamadeen ride past him nodding in his direction once, before coming to a halt.

"Who seeks entry into Ahvasar?" A rough male voice calls out. The speaker high above the city gate is partially hidden from view behind a small battlement.

"Inform Exarch Padua, our uncle, that I am tired of waiting." Rauf surprisingly calls out in a loud and firm voice.

"Rauf!" Isamadeen interjects.

"It's only one of the junior guards. He's bound to run and report to his senior or open the gate." Rauf shrugs his shoulders and gives his brother a mischievous smile.

A moment later, the sliding and grating of a large wooden bar can be heard behind the gate as it slowly creaks open.

A large man with an impressive beard in soldier's attire steps out.

"Young masters Isamadeen and Rauf! It has been a while, welcome." Considering the junior guard who looks peevish, the captain shakes his head, and laughs turning back to face the twins. "Stop teasing my juniors like that or I will lose more of them. There are too few recruits this far from Schiraz."

Isamadeen steps forward, "Apologies Captain Eslan, my brother loves to tease." Isamadeen shakes hands and gives a firm squeeze of the man's left shoulder.

Captain Eslan returns the gesture smiling broadly. "We were not informed of your arrival Isamadeen. The Exarch, your uncle may still be in his room. I will send someone to rouse him."

"May we enter?" Isamadeen turns at Rauf's slightly mocking tone and rolls his eyes.

"Oh. Of course! My manners. Please, come in." The captain gestures us in, then suddenly looking up and shading his eyes from the early morning, exclaims, "General Faruq! I did not expect you. Please, welcome. Is everything well?"

Faruq acknowledges the captain. "Yes Captain. It would be good to rest a while and then seek an audience with the exarch." The captain makes a hurried salute as Faruq walks past.

Leading our horses on foot we make our way through the main gates. I cannot resist a smile at the captain's look of amazement as he now glances between me and Saeed and his emerald green eyes.

Our horses are taken by two young boys and stabled nearby. The captain gives some orders to the young soldier who challenged our entry and sets him running to the large stone structure at the end of the main road.

As Captain Eslan leads us into the heart of the small city, we make our way through the city's still closed markets, the merchants are probably still comfortable in their beds.

With a shock, I recognise the marketplace. Without thinking, my feet and my heart leading, I make my way toward a familiar terrace.

"Azizi? Where are you going?"

I stop mid-step. "I've been here before!" My arms are covered in goosebumps. Turning back to Rauf I call out, "I will join you later."

I take Saeed by the hand, gently guide him beyond the heart of the city, to the terrace that faces the vast expanse of the desert and the rising sun. I sit and pull him down to sit next to me.

I remember the first time, how with much respect and kindness, Hasan had coaxed me into accepting my sexuality. I wrap my arm around Saeed's shoulders and draw him gently to me. He looks at me, a quizzical expression in his brilliant emerald green eyes. And then my heart melts to see him smile, I simply kiss him. He squeezes my hand and looks out with me into the vastness of the desert.

My life seems to have come full circle, joyful excitement rises in my inner being as I now share this place and view with one that

I love dearly. Typically for this region, the colour of the sky splits into three colours. A thin band of deep purple skims the horizon, followed by a larger band of pink and the vast space above mellows to light blue.

I feel the presence before I hear a small discreet cough behind us. Both Saeed and I turn at the same time.

A tall man, dressed in the long robes that I had seen Ijlal wear when he first came to me in the Asfaine mountains, stands gazing intensely at us. His face is narrow, dark brown skin, a nose that ends in a sharp point, a black narrow beard that lengthens his face. He wears the turban typical of some religious sects. His stare is somewhat unsettling.

"Master Azizi?" He briefly looks from Saeed to me. His voice is soft but devoid of emotion. A small chill runs down my spine.

"Yes?" I answer looking directly at him.

"Ah, master Azizi, general Faruq has asked me to take you," he hesitates, briefly glancing at Saeed's hand holding mine, "and your companion to your room and prepare for a meeting with the exarch." The word 'companion' holding a slight question in his tone.

We both stand and without a word wait for him to indicate the way. He bows slightly turning back, leads us towards the large building that rises at the back of the marketplace.

His manner seems awkward, and he often turns to glance at Saeed and me. As we near the building, I sense a tension in him.

"Master Azizi," he bows slightly, "if I may, would you allow me a question?"

I frown before replying, "Yes."

"I have heard great tales of the Sacred Sapphires. Which of the Tears do you hold, Master Azizi?"

My stomach twists in apprehension. *What does he know and how has he come by this knowledge?* Saeed quickly glances at me.

"What is your name in this household?" My question takes him by surprise, he pauses in his steps.

Holding my eyes, he quietly answers, "Vahlen."

My mind quickly runs through the book of names, especially those derived from ancient runes. There is something about the name that suggests a 'veil' or 'secrecy'.

"Thank you, Vahlen. What do you mean by your question?"

He blanches slightly, his eyes drop to the ground. "Forgive me, I did not mean to be rude or intrude."

"Vahlen, your question implies knowledge. How do you come by this kind of information, and is your question to satisfy your curiosity or someone else's?"

Vahlen looks embarrassed, his body tenses. His eyes become shifty, and he looks around furtively as if he has been caught.

"Master Azizi, my apologies." He visibly swallows before going on, "Your name and reputation for defeating the dark sorceress is legendary. The people have never known though whether you kept the Sacred Tear of Apphat or what became of it."

Consciously, I call the sight and take my time to look at his Hala. The intent of the question appears to be genuine; there is a softening of the colours, for want of a better word, a veil shimmers across his Hala.

We reach the lower entrance to the exarch's residence. It has all the hallmarks of a small palace. The building is made up of large light-coloured stones. The corridor we turn into is cool and cleverly lit from small openings in the walls. He pauses in his steps again turning to face us. He takes a deep breath releasing it slowly, he looks around once before speaking in a soft voice. "Master Azizi, I am a loyal servant and will not betray my master the exarch." He pauses a moment then making up his mind he continues, "I can only speak of what is common knowledge. The exarch obtains news quickly. He must maintain the security of the town. Although the city faces the inlet of Malkizar, the city has always been vulnerable from the desert. Many years ago, before the walls were built, it was subject to easy invasion. To this end, my master employs several falconers who train their falcons in his service. These birds regularly bring messages from the major cities of the kingdom."

A slight tense silence follows, Vahlen reflects on what he has just said, no doubt considering whether he has betrayed any confidence.

"A dahé ago, sometime after sunset, one of the falconers brought news from the north. One of the exarch's men had written a hurried message. I only heard a portion of it as it was read." Vahlen pauses unsure whether to go on.

"Vahlen, I may already know what the content of the message was."

He looks at me surprised, then regaining his composure, nods, and resumes.

"There was trouble with the Council of Elders of Naasée. Rumour has it that the Sacred Sapphires were taken from the secret vault and that Prince Elwah has been forced to relinquish his title." Vahlen frowns, "If that rumour is true, then war could be inevitable."

Vahlen looks at me, entreating me to either confirm or deny.

"Vahlen, I respect your loyalty and your honesty. What you say has some truth to it, but the matter is far more complex than what you have just said. We will need to meet with the exarch to explain the situation to him. That is one of the purpose of our arrival here."

We arrive at a door, which Vahlen opens gesturing for me to enter. He turns to Saeed, "I will take you to your room young master."

"Uh, that won't be necessary, we can share this room."

Vahlen looks confused. "I am sorry master Azizi, I was given instructions to accommodate you separately."

I am puzzled and Saeed looks sad. I am about to question those instruction, when a vibrant young voice calls out, "They should not be separated, Vahlen."

Rauf saunters over. "I will take full responsibility, Vahlen. But these two should not be separated; matters of magic and all that." Rauf turns to us and smiles knowingly before turning to Vahlen, still smiling but with a serious expression only Rauf can give.

Vahlen looks a little put out, "Young master Rauf, I, I am not sure. The instructions..."

"Who gave you such instructions, Vahlen?"

The servant is stunned into momentary silence.

"Was it my uncle?"

Vahlen hesitates, shakes his head, and then whispers, "Master Vatsarah."

Rauf immediately raises his upper lip; his brow furrows and he scrunches his nose in an expression of sheer disgust I have never seen on his young face.

"I have never liked that man."

An uneasy feeling fills me. "Rauf? Who is Master Vatsarah?"

"He is my uncle's star caster. His predictions are about as accurate as the weather. He dabbles in magic, and he isn't very good at that either."

Vahlen's expression goes from mild shock to dropping his gaze to the ground.

Rauf puffs up his chest and in a firm voice addresses the servant, "In any case Vahlen, Azizi and Saeed are my guests, they are to share the same room and that is an end to it."

Vahlen bows, his manner suddenly stiff as he turns and walks away.

"Come you two, go in and make yourselves comfortable." Rauf gestures us through the open door.

The room is richly appointed, honey coloured wood panelling covers the lower half of the stone walls. Beautiful, vivid tapestries are hung on opposite sides of a magnificent four poster bed, large enough to easily accommodate two grown men.

Framed with heavy dark blue curtains, a large balcony overlooks the distant desert and the burning sands in the late morning sun. Saeed immediately steps out onto the balcony, admiring the view and taking in deep breaths of the still cool air carrying with it a hint of salt.

I simply stare at Rauf with a new level of puzzled admiration, who unassumingly delights in Saeed's innocent joy.

"It has been a long night Azizi, I should leave you to rest." Rauf turns to leave.

"Not before you reveal to us your true identity as a young noble, Rauf."

I have only ever seen Rauf blush once. His cheeks begin to burn as he gives me a nervous smile. I take a seat at one of the four armchairs that encircle a round table and gesture for him to join me.

There is a soft knock at the door and a young man walks in, eyes downcast, he carries and lays out some delicacies and drinks on the table. Rauf looks up briefly at the young man, "Thank you, Esai." Esai bows before quietly withdrawing.

Rauf consciously avoids eye contact and reaches for a drink. Saeed ambles over and sits next to me, looking expectantly at Rauf.

"Oh... this is unkind! Both of you are making me feel nervous." Rauf takes a sip of his drink, lets a long breath out. "It's not that special really. Our father and his younger brother our uncle, are distant cousins of the Sultan of Schiraz. Uncle Padua was given a minor title of 'Exarch' for protecting the Sultan in a skirmish many years ago. He was then appointed the administrator of Ahvasar."

"Your father is a cousin of the Sultan?" my voice cannot hide my astonishment. "But does that not mean you are related to Ijlal?"

Rauf smiles coyly and blushes. "Second, possibly third cousins." And then he adds, "That is how Ijlal came to call the sons of all the nobles into forming the Companions." Rauf pauses briefly. "Truth be known, Isamadeen and I often suspected that the Sultan prompted his son Ijlal to form the group; a kind of insurance against plots for the throne as well as strengthening the ties between the various nations."

My respect for these young men only deepens.

"And" Rauf adds with a mischievous smile, "it has been fun to roam around the kingdom and generally make mischief." His eyes soften, focussed on some distant memory of an adventure, "As well as taking care of the weak and oppressed."

A playful thought occurs to me. Smiling, I stand to face Rauf who looks up at me enquiringly.

Bowing slightly, "Thank you for your hospitality, your lordship."

Rauf's jaw drops, he blushes and suddenly making admonishing signs with his hands, stands and exclaims, "No, no, no!"

Taking my time to enjoy his reaction, teasing a little more I add, “Now Rauf, I hope you understand. Having been welcomed by the Companions as a brother to you all, how embarrassed I am when either you or Isamadeen, address me as ‘Mahjir.’”

Rauf is a little humbled. He looks down blushing. Looking first to Saeed who looks on with empathy, Rauf turns to me and acknowledges my statement.

“Azizi, yes I understand. Thank you for your brotherly love.”

I go to him raising him and embrace him. Saeed, hungry for the same affection, walks over and wraps his arms around us both.

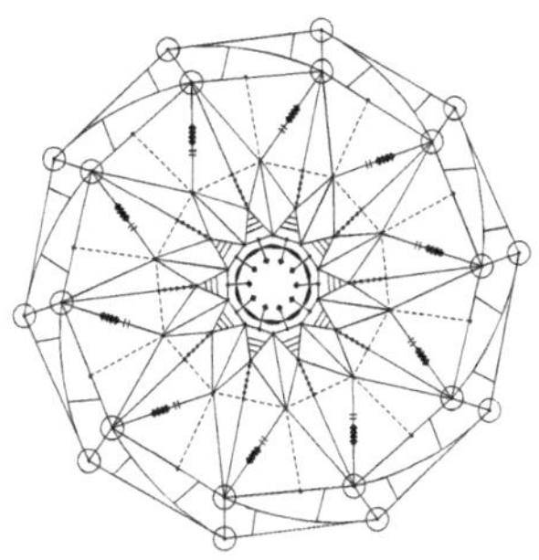

CHAPTER SIX

There is a light knock at the door as it opens, Isamadeen walks in; he pauses briefly, shakes his head, "What am I missing?"

Mischief gilding my words, I answer, "We were reflecting on Rauf's and your noble heritage."

Rauf once more shakes his head, colour flushing his cheeks, "They trapped me into telling them about our uncle and father."

Isamadeen sighs with a sense of resignation and smiles, then suddenly serious, "Rauf did you offend Vahlen? He passed me a moment ago, he looked tense, briefly looked at me and then hurried past."

Rauf looks at us briefly, addressing his twin brother, "He was about to separate Azizi and Saeed and put them in separate rooms."

"Why is that a problem?" Isamadeen shakes his head once more, "You know that Vahlen is head of the household, his responsibility is to make decisions like that."

"Isamadeen!" Rauf exclaims, "You and I both witnessed what Prince Elwah said. Azizi and Saeed are twin souls, they each hold a sacred Tear of Apphat, they should not be separated." Rauf takes a deep breath and adds, "Besides, you and I are twins, when have we ever been apart? Us twins should be together and never separated." Rauf puffs up his chest, glaring directly at Isamadeen.

"Rauf, I understand your motive. I think it was probably more your manner that offended him. You can be very direct sometime, without any thought for social custom. What happens now, if Vahlen makes a complaint to our uncle?"

"He won't. It was not Vahlen's decision. It was advice from master Vatsarah."

Isamadeen's brow furrows slightly.

"What authority does Vatsarah hold that he can make these decisions and instruct, as you say, the head of household to act this way?" Rauf adds with a degree of fervour.

For a moment Isamadeen looks pensive. Finally acknowledging Rauf's statements, "You're right Rauf. I do not know why Vatsarah would give such advice. But next time Rauf," he steps to his twin, first resting his hands on Rauf's shoulders, pulls him closer, "call me and together we can address these issues."

Releasing Rauf, Isamadeen turns to me, "Azizi, you and Saeed have not rested. A meeting will be called shortly with the Exar..., I mean our uncle. There will no doubt be questions to do with our sudden arrival. You may need to prepare for this."

My body suddenly feels weary. "You're right, Isamadeen. We should rest. Will you let us know when the meeting will take place?"

"Yes, of course. It is likely to be after the midday meal. Come Rauf, let them settle and rest. You can catch up with them after the meeting. I am sure Uncle will have prepared an evening meal in honour of our guests." Isamadeen gently places his arm around Rauf's shoulders leading him to the door. Rauf looks back several times before exiting.

Making my way to the inviting bed covered in luxuriously soft covers, I turn to Saeed. He appears preoccupied, frowning slightly. He casually steps to the balcony, inclining his head slightly.

"Saeed?" I call out softly, not wanting to startle him.

He looks back at me, the tension in his face leaves him and he makes his way back inside.

"Azizi, can you hear what I am hearing?"

I listen carefully. The soft murmur of the late morning breeze as it caresses the curtains framing the balcony, the only sound in the room.

"Saeed, what do you hear?"

He shakes his head once, as if to clear his mind.

"It is as if someone is calling my name and the voice is familiar, but I cannot say whose voice it is." His brow furrows again. "It sounds like Master Sahir, but it is different. I do not recognise this voice, but it stirs something inside of me."

A short gust of wind blows in from the dessert, the dark blue curtains billow for a moment, taking the shape of small waves on the ocean of Malkizar. Saeed shivers briefly. My arms are suddenly covered in goose bumps.

"Perhaps I am just tired, and my mind is imagining things." Saeed sighs. He begins to shed his desert clothes and without another word, easily slips into bed. "Azizi, will you lie next to me and hold me until I fall asleep?"

Taking my clothes off, I slip under the covers next to him, the softness of the sheets luring me into almost instant slumber. He rests his head on my shoulder and I listen to his steady breathing as he relaxes. I review the events that have led us to this moment. Another gust of wind catching the top of the clay chimney outside, finds its way through the open window, the slight whistling sound, echoing, resembles a long distant howl.

Large pine trees stand like dark sentinels at the edge of field of snow. A small white mound moves as suddenly blue eyes appear and stare at me.

I wake with a start. Faruq is standing by the bed, small concern in his eyes.

"Azizi? Are you awake?"

My head is heavy. "How long have I been asleep?"

"It is past the midday meal. Food has been brought in, but neither you nor Saeed have touched it."

I look around, Saeed is just stirring next to me, and half raises himself on his elbows. Food and plates are on the round table untouched.

I take a deep breath, taking my bearings. The sky outside the balcony is blazing with light. "Is there some place I can wash?"

Faruq gestures to the far corner of the room where a green curtain hangs. "You will find a large recess in the wall there. The water is not hot, but in this weather, it will be refreshing. There are oils and fresh clothes for both of you."

I throw the covers off, only slightly conscious of my nakedness and yet completely unashamed of Faruq's presence, I make my way and draw the curtain aside. The small room has a small high window, the floor and some of the walls are made of large red clay tiles. In the recess the tiles are highly decorated with various colours and objects that resemble fantastic birds. A large copper plate punctured with small holes is imbedded into the ceiling. A small copper tap protrudes from the wall at waist level. I turn it and immediately a shower of water emerges, for a moment the cold water rushing down my body, almost stops my breath, I let out a small squeal. A few moments of catching my breath, I revel in the refreshing water, reminding me of my mountain streams at the height of season of Elwah.

Moments later, Saeed joins me, initially holding himself with both arms, he steps under the water, laughing, shaking his head, sending out countless droplets of water from his red curls. "We have these in the Huda pass. The water is just as cold!"

I stare at his smooth perfect body, skin as white as sheep's milk, muscles already defining his physique – and then I remember... his naming day. Saeed was born on the second full moon Ayshah in the season of Elwah... it is currently late in the season, so his naming day must be coming up. I remember the crescent moon of Camlac was just over the horizon the previous night. A quick estimate, and relief fills me. His naming day should be in a dahé or two. I will check my calculations later.

I am about to step out to dry myself when his arms wrap around my waist as he pulls me back under the shower.

"Stay a little while more?"

The softness of his skin along the length of my back, the pleading tone of his voice and I struggle to contain my excitement. I turn to gaze into his emerald green eyes, water streaming through his red curls along his shoulders and down his chest.

"Saeed, I am not sure that I could control my feelings if I stay any longer; we would be here for much longer than we should."

He first gives me a quizzical stare, and understanding dawning on him, he smiles a very wicked smile I have not seen before. I try to make light of the situation; I gently push him away. He stares at my obvious arousal and makes a pouting face. This time I laugh out loud and firmly state, “No!”

I dry myself, apply some soothing oils to my body. The oil has a fresh woody fragrance that reminds me of cypress and my mountain forest. I slip into the fresh clothes that have been supplied, feeling the reassuring thick cotton against my skin.

Faruq is seated at the round table, patiently waiting. Looking up, “He hasn’t been initiated?” The directness and implication of the question takes me by surprise. I feel my cheeks burn a little. Faruq senses my awkwardness, “I do not mean to intrude. That was too personal, my apologies.”

“No, he hasn’t. Thank you, Faruq. I forget how comfortable and natural the people of Schiraz are with this subject.” I take a breath, “occasionally I still feel awkward. My people hold very negative views on these things.”

“There is no orange blossom oil...oh.” Saeed steps out, a towel covering part of his body, notices Faruq, stops mid step and blushes.

“You should eat something soon.” Faruq stands and very diplomatically walks to the door, “the Exarch wants to meet with all of us as soon as you are ready.”

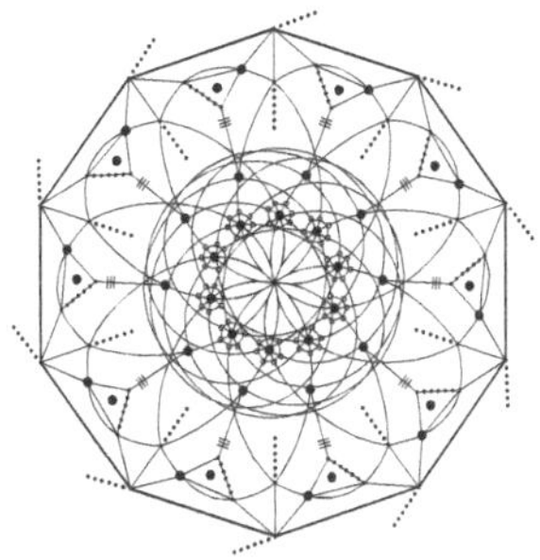

CHAPTER SEVEN

After a quick satisfying meal, we join Faruq along a wide-open columned walkway that makes its way around a beautiful and well-maintained garden. Opened to the sky but enclosed within the confines of the palace, the mixed fragrance and colours of flowers and herbs are a delight to the senses. Even more surprising, given that the city is in the middle of a desert. Obviously, this section of the residence is far from the guest quarters.

Faruq makes a sudden turn, and we enter a long hallway of astounding proportions and décor. The ceiling is much higher, the design much more complex.

We reach a large wooden door engraved with various mythical animals and surrounded by a border of delicately carved flowers. If the door is meant to make a statement of importance, then the next sight leaves me speechless.

We enter a long vast hall. I immediately understand that it is designed to intimidate and announce the wealth and blood line connection to the Sultan of Schiraz.

Tall columns of impressive height and width, the top of which are painted gold, support a magnificent domed ceiling. The central part of the dome is made up of intricately cut clear glass, bathing the hall with natural light. A large colourful rug on the white marble floor leads the eye to a pointed arch, flanked by a pair of drawn curtains. Behind the arch, a large window, similar in shape and design to the arch, looks out onto the blazing white sands of the desert of Keyab.

The air is dry but cool. No doubt the massive sandstone walls that make up the palace, keep the heat of the desert out. There is a subtle fragrance, smoke like, drifting in the air.

Saeed is next to me. I turn to him... "*Azizi.*" His lips haven't moved. I stare at him and answer with my mind, "*Saeed? Can you hear me*?" He nods once, as we both realise with a slight shock that neither has spoken out loud.

I reassure him with my thought, "*We are safe, Saeed. I am with you.*"

Standing at the far end, near one of the columns, Isamadeen and Rauf look to us. Rauf makes a small, timid wave with his hand to Saeed.

"*Azizi*?" Saeed once more turns to me, speaking with his mind, "*What is that scent in the air?*"

I tilt my head up to take a deeper breath, the subtle smoke like fragrance catches at my throat and I almost cough. A vague memory tugs at my senses, a dark shadow passes across my mind and dissolves quickly. A frisson runs up my spine as I briefly recall my experience in the desert at the hands of the murderous Zulfikar, whose name means 'spine cleaver'.

I am uneasy. I begin searching my mind for protection for both of us that does not involve a complex spell or incantation. "I think it may be incense." I reply casually, not wanting to worry him.

"What was that?" Faruq inquires. Realising that I replied out loud, I add, "The smell in the air, I think it is incense." Faruq frowns and nods.

The sun shifts and a shaft of light beams down from the glass dome toward the far end of the arched window. A large figure steps into the light. The first feature that strikes me is his head. Unlike desert people, he does not wear a shemagh. His head is totally bald. The expression of his face is stern and arrogant. The tips of his eyebrows seem fixed in a raised scowl; his generous lips hang down in apparent displeasure. His body belies a gluttonous diet of pleasure eating. He wears soft yellow leather slippers, a long dark, short sleeved robe, open at the front; the collar and front edge are embroidered with a golden design of small leaves of the nakhla tree.

Walking with the aid of an elaborately carved wooden cane, he steps forward pompously and stops, glaring at his nephews before raising his eyes to Faruq.

"General Faruq, there was no word of your visit. Are you on the Sultan's business?"

"Your excellency Padua, we were on our way to Schiraz. It was late, and rather than risk injury to our horses, I decided to take refuge in Ahvasar. I apologise for the lack of advice and any inconvenience." The exarch continues to frown and watch Faruq. "I assure your excellency, that as soon as rested, we will take our leave. I will then convey our gratitude for your kind hospitality to the Sultan."

Padua's face relaxes. The mask of disdain and arrogance begins to crack slightly, and a smile of sorts appears. "Please, general, you honour me too much." His eyes drift finally to Saeed and me. "But you have brought guests – I have never met these individuals." Padua raises an inquisitive eyebrow.

A small figure appears to the left of the exarch. He is slight of build, his face conceals any kind of emotion, but his dark eyes are disturbing, giving off an energy of fierce control.

"My apologies Excellency." Faruq turns to indicate us, "These are my guests and friends. Azizi, from the Asfaine Mountains, and Saeed of the Huda People. A few Duwae ago, both were instrumental in rescuing Prince Shahulm." The exarch's facial expression does not change, but his eyes express a greater interest. "They have been honoured by my father General Giafar and the Sultan himself." As an afterthought, Faruq adds with a tone of vehemence in his voice, "they are under my protection."

The exarch raises both eyebrows, when suddenly Rauf's high pitch voice exclaims, "And they are both our friends and sworn brothers."

The Exarch casually turns to face Rauf, "Nephew, you have such a tendency to speak out of turn."

Rauf blushes slightly, nevertheless, challenges his uncle's glare. Isamadeen whispers something in his brother's ear. Rauf briefly turns to his twin, releases a sigh, and takes a seat near one of the columns with an expression of repressed resentfulness.

"They are welcome of course." The small figure leans to Padua and whispers something. The exarch nods his head, "yes, Master Vatsarah," and quickly raising his hand dismisses him. "In my house, they are of course under my protection and may remain at my leisure."

Faruq's body stiffens a little. "I appreciate your generosity your excellency, but their protection is a duty and a command I will not relinquish."

The exarch casually scratches his left ear with an exaggerated gesture. "Are you suggesting, general, that I would not be able to offer protection in my house?"

Faruq looks momentarily flustered, "Your excellency, that was not my meaning and I apologise for any misunderstanding. The command to protect them is a sworn promise given to those who have authority over me."

There is an awkward pause. The exarch stares at Faruq at first, his face stern and unrelenting, his eyes narrow and casually turning to the small figure, nods once. He turns back to face Faruq, "And who might that be general? Surely not the Sultan my cousin?"

"First and foremost, to Prince Ijlal, my cousin, your excellency and through him, the Sultan; and then to Prince Elwah, regent of Naasée."

A dark look drifts across the exarch's features.

"Prince Elwah? General?" Pausing significantly, he adds, "That is a strange order for his highness to give, considering neither of your guests are from Naasée. How could I verify this command and the reason for giving it?"

Faruq briefly looks tense.

"We heard Prince Elwah instruct Faruq to protect them. That is the reason we..."

The exarch's head whips around at Rauf's interruption and though glaring at his nephew, the exarch's voice is suddenly sweet.

"Nephew, your habit of interrupting should be addressed." Rauf blushes and looks down at his fee. "But, please, Nephew, you say you heard Prince Elwah give this command, so you must have been in his presence, yes?"

Isamadeen makes an audible sigh. "Uncle, please forgive my brother for speaking so bodly; his heart means well but his social decorum is lacking."

"Ah, Isamadeen. Your desire to smooth the way is always refreshing." The exarch smiles benignly and resumes, "Though, Rauf began to give a reason for which you and he were there to hear Prince Elwah instruct general Faruq to protect his guests." It is now Isamadeen's turn to look flustered, his right hand begins to fidget as he gives a harsh look at his twin.

"Your excellency, if I may."

The exarch turns to Faruq, not losing a hint of his smile. If anything, Exarch Padua, a glint in his eyes, looks even more amused.

"Yes, of course general. By all means."

"Your excellency, I was ordered personally by Prince Elwah to safely accompany Master Azizi and Saeed out of Naasée and head to Schiraz." Padua is about to open his mouth and speak, "The order was in writing your excellency and handed to me by the Seeress Mahjira Aïschah."

The exarch nods thoughtfully for a moment. "And general, do you still have this written order?"

"The parchment was immediately consumed by elf fire the moment I read it."

"Oh." Padua's face has lost none of its amusement. "How convenient!"

The air goes still and tight. The star gazer Vatsarah shares his master's amusement, allowing himself to smile behind his hand. He leans once more to the exarch, whispering something.

"You see general, Although I am master of this city, I have my own orders." Padua pauses a moment.

"One of those orders is to protect this city and its people. That order comes from the Sultan himself." Padua allows the silence to fill the room before going on. "General, there are too many inconsistencies. For instance, are you able to tell me where Prince Elwah is?"

"Your excellency, if he is not in Naasée, then I cannot."

Faruq's response strikes me as clever and one that has already anticipated the exarch's line of reasoning.

After a considered pause, the exarch begins again, "I have it on good report, General, that he is not in Naasée. In fact, from the reports I received during the night, Naasée is in a bit of disorder."

Sensing that he is about to be caught in well laid out trap, Faruq, having discerned that the exarch knows more than he is letting on, falls silent.

An unsettling feeling simmers in my gut. I should have thought of telling Faruq about what Vahlen told me, specifically the spies that send out messages by hawks. A hawk would have arrived at the city well before us.

"Your excellency is well informed. No doubt your trained hawks fly even by night."

Of course, Faruq would know, as a general serving a prince and the Sultan himself, he would be well informed of the techniques princes and administrators employ to stay abreast of events. After all, Ijlal his prince has the power to transform into a great kestrel.

"Yes, general, they do." The fact Faruq knows of his spies does not for one moment ruffle his demeanour.

"General, let me get to the point. Please let me know if I go too fast, or if anything I say is either unknown to you or if you disagree." Padua pauses, and I cannot help but think that he does it for effect. I notice Rauf and Isamadeen have both become very still and quiet.

"You see general, I know that Prince Elwah is not in Naasée. In fact, it appears that he has left the city altogether, and in the company of the Captain of the Royal guards." Pausing for further effect in the guise of allowing Faruq to disagree, he continues, "I have further information that the Great Council of Magicians is in disarray." Taking a breath, and focussing his eyes on Faruq, "rumour has it, general, that the reason Elwah is no longer in the city, is that he is no longer in possession of the Sacred Tear of Apphat. As such he has been forced to relinquish his title."

Again, the exarch pauses, allowing Faruq to respond. Faruq remains silent and offers no reply.

"This is where my reports become interesting, general." Exarch Padua briefly glares at Rauf, who fidgets in his seat. He then raises his eyes to me and Saeed before returning his attention to Faruq. "The reports also mention that two individuals, magicians if the reports are to be trusted, have left Naasée. It also states that some senior members of the Council have ordered the apprehension and return of these individuals back to Naasée."

Faruq turns momentarily to me, his posture straightens, although he exudes power and calm, his countenance suggests a hint of uncertainty edged with determination. He turns back to face the exarch.

"And so, in the early dawn, you, general Faruq, arrive in the company of my useless nephews, and accompanied by two individuals, whose eyes and bearing would indicate magic."

Faruq remains silent. His left hand tightens around the hilt of his short sword, a gesture that does not go unnoticed by the exarch.

"Do you understand the position you have left me in? I appreciate your role as protector, it appears to me that you have fulfilled your command. Now it is left to me to decide what to do with your two guests. Should I return them to Naasée as instructed by the Great Council? So far, all I have is the certainty that this could lead to war. My city is vulnerable general. I will not allow the politics of Naasée to demolish the peace I have fought hard to achieve."

"Excellency, that is precisely the reason I was given the command to protect Azizi and Saeed. They are to be kept away from Naasée until Prince Elwah calls for them."

The doors of the great hall are suddenly flung open, and a good two dozen fully equipped soldiers enter briskly and position themselves around us and Faruq.

"Excellency? What is the meaning of this?" Cold outrage guilds Faruq's voice, his hand further tightens on the hilt of his sword.

"It is easy to understand general. It appears that the two individuals you have brought into my city, are fugitives wanted by the Great Council of magicians of Naasée. One question is why – what makes them so valuable to a Council of Elders that have the reputation for non-action in the face of peril? And then of course is the other question – you have already mentioned the name of one of your guests – Azizi. This surely must be the renowned Azizi who single handed was able to defeat the Evil one? According to stories, exaggerated no doubt, that he is in possession of one if not both Tears of Apphat.

You understand now, how as ruler of this city, it is up to me to warrant its protection. If it comes to war, then the possession of one who holds the Tears of Apphat is my guarantee of victory in war and an assurance of peace?"

The exarch stands to his full height, "it is simple general Faruq, they are not to leave my city without my authorisation."

There is brief pause, before the outraged voice of Rauf exclaims: "Uncle! You would make them prisoners?"

Padua turns nonchalantly to his nephew, "Ah, Rauf it is good to see that you are not as dim-witted as I thought."

Raising his eyes to me and Saeed, "You will be well looked after, but you will be taken to different quarters to ensure both your comfort and my security."

Exarch Padua briefly gestures to the soldiers, "you have your orders."

A soldier steps forward to Faruq and attempts to disarm him. In one gesture, Faruq drops the man to his knees, draws his sword, points it at the man's throat. Four soldiers immediately surround Faruq pointing their swords at him. He reluctantly releases his weapon and follows the soldiers out.

I turn briefly as Isamadeen's voice cuts through the tumult, "Uncle, this action can only lead to war!"

"Nephew, you are a little smarter than your twin. Think. I hold general Faruq – cousin to Prince Ijlal and the only son of General Giafar. I hold Azizi reputed to hold one of the Tears of Apphat, which assures my victory in any war; and then Isamadeen, I hold you and your twin for good measure – apart from Ijlal, you two are the sons of my brother who is second in line to the throne of Schiraz, I have my assurances. You see dear nephews, it has been a while in the planning, but this, this...” gesturing to encompass the soldiers taking us away, “this is a gift. In the realms of royalty and war, even nephews are expendable.”

I steal one last look at the twins, before being shoved through the doorways. Rauf is a picture of distress and outrage, Isamadeen looks on bewildered as soldiers surround them and take their short swords away.

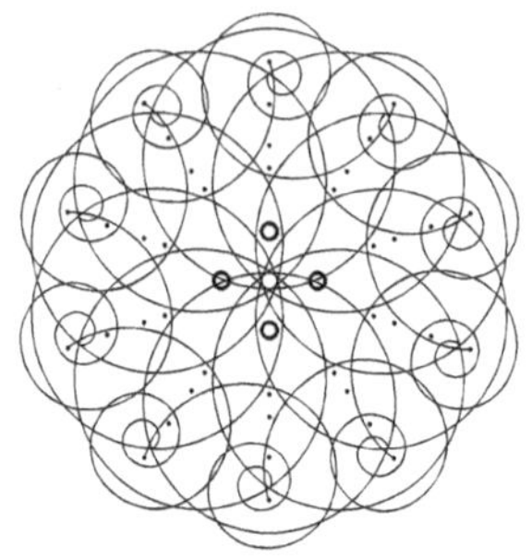

CHAPTER EIGHT

We are escorted down a different hallway to the one we took this morning. My head is still reeling with the speed of events that have just taken place with the exarch.

Occasionally one of the soldiers gives one of us a shove forward, urging us to move on at a quicker pace. Their swords still drawn, some of them look askance at Saeed and me, and at least one of them shows fear in his eyes.

A small person ahead of us, quickly makes way by retreating into the arch of a doorway. His eyes wide with fear and astonishment, I recognise the young boy who had brought us food earlier on.

Faruq and Saeed walk in ahead of me. I am thrust through a door of a large but dimly lit room. Faruq momentarily glares at the last soldier who quickly averts the stare and hurriedly shuts the door, locking it from the outside. A stern order is given, indicating that at least two soldiers are posted on the outside.

Faruq has begun to prowl, a look of focussed fury etched on his features. On the occasion that he looks at me, his piercing blue eyes have gone cold.

"I am truly sorry Azizi. I did not foresee this. His misplaced aspiration to the throne has come as a complete surprise." Faruq resumes his slow pacing, his forehead creased, fixated on an internal dialogue.

Sudden, angry raised voices and scuffling noises increase outside the door.

"Get your filthy hands of me!" Rauf's sudden enraged voice commands, followed by a loud muffled swear word from one of the soldiers.

The front door opens abruptly as first, Isamadeen is pushed forward, then Rauf is forcefully thrown through the open door, making him stumble to the ground. I take stock of the three soldiers that were required to manoeuvre Rauf; one of them has a swollen red eye, which will no doubt ripen to purple, another is still swearing under his breath, holding his abdomen in obvious pain, the third rubs his left wrist, as if sprained. How Rauf, one head smaller than me, managed to deliver such injuries, makes me smile. I remember then, the swiftness and calculating fighting ability that he and the companions had demonstrated, when we first stormed the Great Citadel of the Overlord.

Isamadeen helps his twin to stand. Rauf in his inimitable manner, with great disdain makes to brush dust off himself.

"Rauf, I don't think it will help our cause," Rauf glares at his brother, "but thank you, I wanted to do something much worse." Rauf smiles back weakly.

Saeed steps up to Rauf, "Were you hurt?"

Making a scoffing noise, Rauf replies, "No, but one of them will be nurturing his manhood for some time." The tension is released, I cannot help chuckle at the vehemence and ruthless tone of the remark, coming from such an angelic face.

A moment of stunned stillness follows.

"Faruq," Isamadeen's low, composed voice breaks the silence; "I, we had no knowledge that our uncle was planning such a thing against the Sultan." Faruq stops pacing. "Otherwise, we would not have come here."

"It is not your fault Isamadeen. In any case, I made the decision to stop here the night."

Faruq takes a few steps, then turning back to Isamadeen, "Do you know where in the city palace we are?"

Isamadeen looks at Rauf who walks over to the only window at the far end of the room, "The east tower!" Isamadeen nods in agreement, "it faces the harbour of Malkizar and," adding with a sigh as if reading Faruq's mind, "it's a long way up."

Faruq makes his way to the window that has three vertical metal bars across it, peers down, steps back and affirms. "Yes. It is." As an afterthought, "We need a plan. Rauf, are you very familiar with this side of the palace?"

"Yes." Both Isamadeen and Rauf answer. "We used to play here as children, finding all the secret rooms."

Isamadeen briefly looks up to Faruq, then hanging his head, "This room is one of the most secure, there are no secret doors or escape tunnels. There is only one entrance, the one we came through." Adding with a sour note, "perfect for keeping prisoners."

A despondent silence hangs in the room. The occasional movement of air through the barred window, as the desert breeze begins to shift to the sea, whispers hopeless words in the room.

"Azizi?" Faruq's whispered plea breaks the silence. Knowing what he is about to ask, a small knot forms in my stomach, "Azizi, is there anything that you or Saeed can do?"

Saeed glances at me, a look of hope in his eyes. As casually as I can, not wanting to give false hope, I stand up and amble to the window. I stare out at a small expanse of sand, the shadow of the tower we are in, stretching out like a long finger to the dark blue waters of Malkizar; a large gulf where two ships of considerable size are moored. My heart is pounding to see the waters so close and the possibility of escape. "I didn't realise we were so close to water," I turn to Faruq, who stares back and inclining his head frowns inquiringly.

"Do you think...?" Faruq whispers.

"I don't know, but it is interesting." Facing Saeed, "Saeed, would you come and look at this?"

Saeed strides over, gazes out and then gives me a questioning look.

"Saeed, when you look at the water, do you sense anything?"

He stares back at the view, takes a few deep breaths, and responds in a dreamy tone, "I feel calm and a little excited, as if I am seeing a friend."

"Mmm." I nod in acknowledgement. "The water in the gulf there, is of the ocean Malkizar."

For a moment, Saeed's look of comprehension is quickly followed by a stunned expression of mild fear.

A brittle silence hovers over the room.

Rauf and Isamadeen have stood up, a quiet air of anticipation filling their features. My skin is suddenly covered in goose bumps.

"To answer your question Faruq, there are several possibilities."

I allow my mind to relax and let my instinct speak. "Most of the structure of this town, including its defensive wall is made of wood; a long time ago, there must have been a large forest in this place." My voice is grave, not quite the voice of the Great Spirit that once spoke through me, "I could so easily call up the element of fire that would destroy it. Saeed could certainly call the Nācken of Malkizar, extinguish the flames and flood this town, turning it into marshlands, leaving this tower the only feature of its past. It would become known as the tower of doom, the land around it, cursed and empty." I am aware of the awe that suddenly fills their features. Even Saeed has gone very still, his face paling slightly. I take a deep breath, "That action would probably cause the deaths of many innocent people in this town, including those that simply followed orders and currently guard this room."

Faruq stares at me, realising the consequence of misusing the power of the Sacred Tears.

"Faruq, your sword was taken from you, but they did not take your spirit nor your strength as a general." Like the falling snow of my hometown, a gentle energy settles over me, "the strength and power of the Sacred Stones of Apphat is secret and it remains. It works in mysterious ways. There is no need to call for its destructive aspect. It is at work now. We will wait patiently for it to manifest."

The moment passes, the faint echoes of a voice I have known fades away. The silence of the room returns.

There is a rattle at the door, unlocked, the young servant Esai walks in with eyes downcast, carrying a tray of food and drinks. He briefly stops, looks around and finally decides to set the tray on the only wooden table in the centre of the room.

"Esai?" The young boy looks up at Rauf and smiles shyly.

"Make haste!"

Rauf's head whips around at the rough command from one of the soldiers at the door, who involuntarily steps back at Rauf's glaring eyes.

As Esai lays down the food, he catches Rauf's attention, "Master Rauf, these came straight from the kitchen." Esai taps one of the bowls containing small portions of cooked meat, and subtly shakes his head. Rauf looks at the content, gazes back at Esai and nods.

Esai bows and quietly leaves. The door is shut firmly, and the lock clatters into place.

"What was that exchange Rauf?" Faruq inquires.

"Do not eat these," pointing at the meat dish, "they have been tampered with or poisoned."

Saeed pales visibly and retreats away from the food.

All eyes are on the food. Each wondering what dishes are safe. Rauf's stomach groans loudly, relieving some of the tension.

"Well, I'm hungry." Rauf picks up a piece of cheese made from sheep's milk and taking a bite, declares "Azizi," making an effort to speak and chew, "if am to die from this, avenge my death and burn this tower down!"

For a long moment, everyone stares at Rauf, expecting the worst. Rauf tears a piece of bread from the fresh loaf and starts to chew, smiling cheekily.

"Rauf is right!" all eyes turn to me. "Only the meat is corrupt. It gives off a dark energy."

It takes no time at all for hunger to break our inhibitions, and carefully moving the dish that contains the meat far away, we take our time to eat the rest of the dishes and drink the water provided.

"We should throw away this meat and make them think that we have eaten it." Faruq states, a calculating tone in his voice.

I scan the room once more, aware of a small recess, which I assume opens into a small space that holds a toilet and washbasin.

"Can we throw it in the toilet?"

"Yes, but make sure not to clean the dish. It has to look as though we have simply eaten it."

Rauf returns with the empty dish, replacing it on the table and asks, "But will they not suspect something is amiss, if we are still conscious? We do not know what the intent was – to kill us or render us unconscious?"

Isamadeen cuts in, "It is likely not to take immediate effect."

Rauf stares at his brother. "How do you know that?"

"If I know our uncle, he will not be in a rush. He will have carefully considered all his options and what leverage he can use to manipulate the situation to his advantage. Our deaths would not have the same weight as us alive. It is also possible that if it is poison and not a drug, that he holds the antidote to reverse the effect. In any case he wants to hold all the most favourable elements."

Faruq stirs from his contemplation, "I think you're right Isamadeen."

The sudden rattle of the lock makes me jump. The door opens allowing Esai in. He briefly scans the room, taking each one of us in turn and moves to the table. He suddenly stops, his outstretched hands begin to tremble as he stares at the empty bowl.

Rauf realises Esai's dilemma and ambles over. "Thank you Esai, the meat was a little unusual but tasty."

Esai visibly pales, stares at Rauf who gives him a wink and a subtle shake of his head.

Esai releases a brief breath, picks up the tray and eyes downcast leaves the room. The door does not shut behind him, instead two large soldiers step in, blocking the exit. The older one points at Rauf and Isamadeen and in a gruff tone, commands,

"You, both of you. You are to come with me!"

Rauf immediately pales, stares at Isamadeen who stands and glaring at the soldiers, replies, "On whose order?"

The soldier steps forward and raises his hand, his intention to strike is short lived as Saeed unexpectedly steps in between, his eyes blazing an emerald fury that suddenly lights up the room. The soldier takes several steps back finally lowering his arm, quickly steps out of the room and slams the door shut. The lock hurriedly rattles into place.

As if a thunderstorm had just broken out, the air is filled with a prickling sensation. The intensity in Saeed's eyes fades. The room returns to dim shadow.

"Thank you, Saeed." Isamadeen whispers in awe.

Rauf tentatively sidles up to Saeed, and then throws his arms around him. "Thank you, Saeed."

"Perhaps, they will think twice now." Faruq's mildly amused tone dispels the tension. He resumes a slow pace around the room.

Stepping to Saeed, I lean in and whisper, "Have you regained control, Saeed?"

He nods, I notice his clenched fists by his side still shaking with his fury. I place my arm around his shoulders and whisper, "Take some deep breaths, Saeed. It will pass."

He acknowledges me, slowly makes his way to the far side of the room, and sits on the ground, leaning his back to the wall. He stares at his fists, slowly releasing them. Saeed looks up at me, the quiet trust in his eyes and expectation of a solution, equally endears me and frightens me.

I make my way to the window.

The light outside the barred window is darkening. The sun setting on the opposite side of the tower, casts long shadows of the buildings along the sand toward the gulf of Malkizar. The pointed roof of the tower's shadow already reaches beyond the edge of the water, wavering with the ripples lapping at the shore.

The sky fades to a dark cerulean blue. Bright stars appear one after the other. The light in the room fades quickly, dark shadows fill the corners. A deepening silence settles in the room; Rauf and Isamadeen sit on the ground next to each other. Faruq has stopped pacing, instead leaning against the stone wall next to the window, an intense look of brooding concentration fixed on his face.

Some time passes, Rauf gently leans his head on his brother's shoulder and closes his eyes, steadying his breathing, his hands have relaxed into his lap.

A light behind me makes me turn back to the darkening sky. The crescent moon of Camlac has grown to almost half its surface. Suddenly, loud, and clear, the howl of a wolf is carried on the breeze. Saeed stands up and rushes to the window, stares at me. My arms are covered in goose bumps; Elwah's words echoing in my mind.

Some shuffling noise outside the door distracts me out of my thoughts.

The door opens cautiously. One of the soldiers stands nervously on the threshold, scanning the room before stepping back. A man, slight of build dressed in a drab dark robe steps forward. His neutral face conceals any kind of emotion, hair around his face hangs in black oily strands but his dark eyes are disturbing, giving off an energy of fierce control. I recognise the man who kept whispering to the exarch at our meeting. Vatsarah holds a large wooden staff, atop of which is a large clear crystal. He carries it as if it has the power to protect him. His eyes keep shifting from openly staring at Saeed, briefly looks at me and then stares at Faruq with a condescending smirk.

"One of the exarch's soldiers has complained that one of you has used magic to stop him in his duties." Even his voice is greasy, laden with disdain.

"If you call striking one of the Sultan's cousins without cause or provocation a duty Vatsarah, then that soldier needs to be whipped." Rauf's angry tone and fierce eyes challenge the star gazer.

Vatsarah smirks briefly to himself. Raising his hand in an apparent air of contrition, his tone of voice suddenly sweet, "Master Rauf, I am indeed dismayed to hear this. I come to beseech you all to understand my master's mind. I disapprove of the way you have been treated and have declared this to the exarch."

Rauf's short snort of contempt interrupts Vatsarah who briefly attempts to ignore it.

"Master Azizi," he turns his dark eyes toward me, for a moment his gaze seems to falter. Straightening himself, he reasserts a level of certainty. "You have met Vahlen, the head of his excellency's household?"

I nod, suspicious of his question. "We have met him briefly."

"Mmm," Vatsarah makes an amused expression. "When he questioned you and your purpose here, and the fact that the Sacred Sapphires had disappeared from the secret location in Naasée, Vahlen assures me that you did not deny this, in fact you affirmed that this was the reason you came here. Which leads me to believe, that you still hold at least one of the Sacred Tears. This has to be the reason the Council of Elders have requested that you return to them."

I simply glare at him, which eventually makes him nervous. Taking a breath, he seems to want to change the course of the conversation.

"His excellency seems to think that possession of one of the Sacred Tears, would guarantee him success in all his endeavours." Pausing more for effect, he resumes, "as a fellow magician, master Azizi, I know how dangerous that would be. The exarch does not have the magical power to hold one of those. It would either destroy him, or the stone would simply split or shatter in his hand."

I do not respond to his statement, which in turn exacerbates him.

"You, especially since you have wielded the power of the stones, you are in danger." Looking around at the others, he adds, "All of you are in danger. The exarch will not relinquish his desire. I am here to offer a solution, which would see all of you leave unharmed and in peace."

It is my turn to smile at him. "Please, explain your plan."

"Master Azizi, if you were to leave the stones in my care until such time as would be convenient to return them to you, then I cannot see the exarch holding you and your friends any longer."

I can't help myself and I make a small, amused noise. His demeanour stiffens.

"Vatsarah? That is your name, am I correct?"

His mouth stiffens into a straight unyielding line. "Yes."

'First, Vatsarah, I find your request offensive. The goddess Ishtar herself entrusted me with the Sacred Tear. It also amuses me that you assume that the Tear of Elwah is actually on my person." His eyes wander over me, almost in an obscene way, and then begins to scan the room for any parcels or packages.

His attitude changes again. I perceive the energy of anger growing in him.

"Then if it is not on your person, have you relinquished it to another?" Pointing at Saeed, who has stood up and glares back at Vatsarah. "Perhaps you friend over there, with the magical green eyes?"

Vatsarah cannot hold Saeed's angry stare, the energy in his emerald eyes more than a challenge for the stargazer's assertiveness.

Turning back to me, "Master Azizi," the words almost spat with disdain, "you are far too young and inexperienced in these matters. You should leave the politics of this land to those who know how to handle them. I demand that you release the stones to me! If you will not do so willingly, then there are other methods." Muttering some sounds, he straightens his staff before him. By a trick of the light, or a very basic incantation, the crystal adorning the top of his staff begins to glow. Saeed and the others step back, unsure.

I stand my ground, leveling my eyes and meet his with utter defiance. An image of a blue butterfly briefly appears in my mind. His staff means nothing to me. It has no power in the world, his threat is an empty one. I extend my hand and whisper a command "Ta-ela Li!" As soon as spoken, the staff flies out of his grasp and into my outstretched hand.

His arm still extended; he simply gapes at his empty hand.

I whisper a further incantation, "Yahraqu!" The staff immediately bursts into spontaneous flames, I release it as it falls into a small pile of ash on the ground, the crystal shattering into small shards turning grey as they lie lifeless.

Vatsarah cannot hide his astonishment, fear floods his features, he unwillingly steps back.

"Vatsarah, did you really think it would be that simple?" He hasn't stopped gaping; walking backwards, his hand reaches out feeling for the door frame. A soldier still stands at the threshold, his eyes fixed in terror with what he has just witnessed. "Tell your master, the exarch what has occurred here and inform him that his demise is not far away. The signs will manifest themselves at the height of the moon of Camlac tonight."

Not daring to turn his back, Vatsarah makes a hasty retreat. The door closes firmly and the lock rattles once more into place.

CHAPTER NINE

"Master Azizi, I do not think that you have made a lifelong friend."

Faruq's dry sense of humour provokes an amused snort from Rauf and Isamadeen. Saeed is still staring at me in awe.

"How did you... what was...?" Saeed's whispered questions only affirm his astonishment. For the twins, although taken by the speed at which the events took place, simply nod their heads in acknowledgment of what they have seen in the past. To them, this is almost expected, I hear their thoughts – *'do not challenge one who speaks with the authority of the Great Spirit'*.

"Saeed, the answer is simple. I am sure that you sensed that Vatsarah's power is limited to tricks and basic incantations. His threat was simply a bluff misplaced with his sense of self-importance. Although his staff is an instrument of magic, even a crude one, both the wood that came from trees and the crystal dug from the earth, responded to the guardian of nature that lies within my power. Both elements of earth, together with the power of the Sacred Stone of Elwah, answered and acknowledged my command." Saeed's brow creases slightly, in response I add, "yes Saeed, in a sense they appeared to be destroyed, but they were willing to sacrifice themselves to release the negative energy that Vatsarah had imbued into them and return to a natural state."

The twins' wonder does not diminish with that explanation.

"Azizi?" I turn to Faruq, whose face still holds concern. "Azizi, Vatsarah obviously has a strong hold on the exarch and his decision-making process. Although the exarch may decide not to directly challenge you or Saeed, I think he will only increase the level of security around us. They may again wish to split us up."

"I will not allow them to do so." My assertion obviously relieves him of that concern.

"Azizi, I understand that you cannot use your power in ways that would harm innocents. What we need then, are soldiers." It is obvious that my godmother's words to him in the cave of Gibrar, did not go unheeded. I wait for him to continue. "Azizi, do you think you could contact prince Ijlal?"

Yes! Of course! Ijlal could easily raise an army and if not, he certainly could convince Shahulm to raise one. Contacting my godmother and Elwah had always been such an easy task for me, the link based on personal and mutual energies of magic making it almost instantaneous.

"Yes, that at least I think I can do."

I need a focus, flames, but there is nothing here to start a fire.

"Saeed?" Looking keenly at me, he stands beside me. "Saeed, I need a focus to make a calling. I have always used the flames of a fire to do so. Setting this room on fire would put all of us in danger." Understanding dawns on him. "I need to you to call the fire and hold it alight for as long as you can until I complete the calling to Ijlal."

Taking a deep breath, gratitude in his eyes for the trust I am placing in him, he nods his head in acknowledgement.

"Do you remember the incantation I taught you in the desert?"

"Yes, Azizi. I do."

"This time however you will need to focus your attention to the air between us. There is nothing here that should be burnt, the air itself and the power of your mind will maintain it."

Seriousness fills his features, and he nods once more in agreement.

I sit on the cold stone ground and Saeed lowers himself opposite me, his emerald green eyes fixed on mine.

"Saeed, please begin."

Saeed cups his hands in front of himself. His eyes focus on the space over them. I watch as his mind forms the idea of fire and slowly, his will echoes with the calling of *Narun,* the name of fire.

I must remember Ijlal in my mind. I stare into the flames that flicker above Saeed's hands. Slowly, I conjure the face I remember from my dream that haunted me night after night in the duwae of my sixteenth naming day. Dark eyes look at me, a haunting echo whispers, *'he is so beautiful'*. My mind is filled with Ijlal's face.

All at once, I see him as if he were standing before me. He was about to retire for the night, astonishment mixed with the pleasure of seeing me fades as he frowns.

"Azizi?"

"Yes, Ijlal. I do not have much time. Please listen carefully. Faruq, the twins, Saeed, and I have been imprisoned by the Exarch of Vatsarah. I believe he is planning to use us to overthrow the rule of your father, the Sultan." I see astonishment gradually replaced with cold anger mounting in him. "Ijlal, I will do everything I can to protect them, but my power is limited, I am forbidden to use force against those who do not have magic." As an afterthought I add, "I have dealt with the exarch's magician, he is no longer a threat."

In the manner of a true commander, he comes to a decision with determination.

"I will gather the Companions and a contingent of Royal Guards to leave tonight." Frowning slightly, "Can you hold until morning?"

Even at 'desert speed', as Saeed used to say, it will take Ijlal and his men until morning to arrive.

"Yes, Ijlal. Be aware though, the exarch has spies in every town. They are hawk trainers that send messages back to him." I withdraw my energy as the image of him begins to fade, I see him hurrying out of his rooms with purpose.

"Saeed, it is done, you can withdraw your will from the fire."

Taking a deep breath, Saeed closes his eyes for a moment and folds his hands together; the flames abate, leaving only the cold air of the night.

Rauf in his inimitable fashion, sits next to Saeed and places an arm around his shoulders. Saeed relaxes, the effort obviously a stress on his untrained mind and body.

"Were you able to contact him?" Faruq anxiously asks.

"Ijlal is gathering the Royal guards and the rest of the companions and is leaving this night. He should be here by morning."

Faruq relaxes, but the tension does not completely leave him. He resumes his pacing.

Suddenly, howls of several wolves call out to the moon of Camlac. We all stare at each other. Saeed looks at me with wonder, whispering, "It has called its tribe."

"Yes, Saeed. Prince Elwah said that if it senses danger to you or me, it would appear."

The wolves have gathered in obvious large numbers and continue to howl outside the city gates. The light of the moon of Camlac, which at first painted long strands of light through the window, continues to rise, shortening those into pale small squares of bright white against the cold stones. It must be nearing its highpoint. The howls of the wolves increase, creating a loud and eerie atmosphere.

What seems like ages has passed, the wolves have not relented with their call to the moon of Camlac.

A strong male voice calls out a brief and loud command. The lock rattles, and the door is flung open.

A large man, dressed in a senior officer's attire enters, briefly looks around. I recognise him as the captain who met us at the city gates the previous dahé. He finally focusses his attention on Faruq who has remained seated on the ground looking impassively at the visitor.

"Captain Eslan? To what do we owe the pleasure of your presence?"

The captain flinches at Faruq's obvious sarcastic tone. He straightens himself, "General Faruq," taking a deeper breath, "I will not pretend that you are not deeply offended at the way you have been treated. I am not privy to the discussions of the generals and the Exarch. It is probably too late to say that I was completely unaware of the politics the exarch was playing."

Faruq maintains his neutral stare. Captain Eslan begins to tense a little.

"Captain, I do not know whether to be offended at your assertion or simply mildly amused with your naiveness." Before the captain has a chance to respond, Faruq adds, "even the lowest soldier will have heard rumours and formulated certain conclusions."

The captain visibly pales, fidgets a moment.

"So, captain, are you here to free us or simply to make sure that we are, as the exarch assured us, of 'being well looked after?'" Faruq holds up a hand to stop Eslan from speaking, "which includes making sure that we are offered food that has been poisoned?"

The captain pales even more, looks at each one of us, an unmistakable look of panic in his eyes.

"Poison? General, I don't, I know nothing of poison! What do you mean?"

Faruq allows himself a low chuckle. "Captain, this does nothing to recommend your abilities to me as a trusted officer of the exarch's army."

An awkward and frosty pause ensues.

"General Faruq, I assure you that I know nothing of poison. That is not the way I would ever treat prisoners, any prisoner." He adds vehemently, "Even if ordered."

A loud chorus of wolf howls fills the chamber. Captain Eslan visibly shudders.

"That places me in a strange position of wanting to believe you, Captain." The last word uttered with the smallest hint of aloofness.

Looking directly at the captain, Faruq adds, "it is fortunate for us that we have not one but two talented magicians with us."

The captain awkwardly glances at Saeed and then me.

Bowing his head, he drops his voice slightly above a whisper, "I heard what occurred with Vatsarah." Raising his head slightly, "I can truly say that I am glad."

"Oh?" Faruq's scorn has not diminished.

"General, I do not like the man, and he has too much influence on the exarch." He adds quickly, "No one here has the authority or courage to challenge Vatsarah. Least of all a mere captain."

Faruq does not say anything, his unbroken stare at the captain speaking volumes.

The sky is darkening, shadows begin to fill the corners of the room, the small pale squares of the moonlight have all but disappeared. A single wolf howl is quickly followed by another chorus of wolves. It seems that the pack has grown, and the sound appears to come from various directions. Captain Eslan shudders once more.

"General, I do not know anything of magic. The guards on the city walls have reported increasing number of wolves that have gathered around the city walls. No one dares to step outside the city. They report that a single large white *fanak* leads the pack. The sight and sound of so many desert wolves is unheard of in our history. The soldiers are beginning to lose their nerves. These men are superstitious at best, magic unsettles them." Eslan pauses briefly. "I come to ask if your magicians can do something to either dispel their fear or somehow make the wolves leave?" Eslan looks edgy.

"That is not something I can control, Captain." Faruq looks amused, "You will need to address your request to Master Azizi or Saeed directly."

The captain turns to me bows slightly and is about to repeat his question, I interrupt him. "Captain, the white 'fanak' you refer to, has already killed a notorious assassin. I witnessed as it tore the man's head off in one movement." My words only heighten the man's nervousness. "This white wolf has dedicated its loyalty to safeguard Saeed and me from potential harm."

Eslan looks like his legs are about to give way.

"It followed us here from Naasée. When we did not appear after entering the city, it must have sensed that our safety was compromised. It reacts in the only way it knows. But know this, captain, if this wolf gains entry to your city, nothing and no one will stand in its way, until it has secured our wellbeing."

To my astonishment, the man's hand surreptitiously makes the sign to ward off witchcraft. The gesture, seen so often amongst the villagers of Asfaine, so infantile in its intent almost makes me smile.

"No matter what you wish for captain," he suddenly straightens the fingers of his hand, "if magic is required, it will have its way; either the magic of nature or that of mankind."

Eslan drops his chin in what appears to be a brief bow. He is about to turn, "Master Azizi, I do not have much influence with the exarch. I want to protect my men from harm." He hesitates a moment, "I do not have the authority to release you. To do so will end my life and place yours in greater danger. I am merely following orders." He lets out a long sigh.

"Captain," Faruq looks upon Eslan with a degree of comprehension, "following orders is something I understand. However, even as a captain there comes a time when an order given goes so much against your sense of duty as a man, that you need to question that order."

He turns once on his feet and steps toward the door, "Captain," Faruq's voice stops him, and he turns back. "Captain, was it your decision to come to us just now?"

Eslan briefly looks down at the ground, raising his eyes to meet Faruq, "In part it was. The men have become anxious to the point where I fear they will no longer follow my orders. They could blindly follow the orders from the exarch who will make decisions based on Vatsarah's advice. If they perceive that..." he pauses swallowing hard, glimpses briefly at me, "if the soldiers perceive that Master Azizi is the cause of this event, they may in their superstitious stupidity attempt to kill the source of such magic."

A cold shudder runs through me. Being called a witch's brat as a child, beaten for having visions, is suddenly nothing compared to being threatened with death. I find myself standing, confronting Eslan. A current of hot air rises up my spine, my vision blurs momentarily. I take a deep breath to regain control, but it is too late, the power in my eyes is glowing a vibrant blue. Eslan takes several steps back, only the wall at his back stops him.

"Believe me captain, although I have sworn never to use magic to protect myself from harm, I cannot guarantee that I would restrain myself from preventing harm to my friends."

"I have sworn no such oath." Saeed stands beside me, his attitude challenging. "I will stand beside Azizi and protect him with all my might." His words spoken with such power that my body is suddenly covered in goose bumps. Saeed's eyes are again glowing a bright green.

"And so will we!" Rauf, Isamadeen and Faruq stand beside me and Saeed.

Captain Eslan visibly gulps, stares blindly at us and without another word, hurriedly steps out of the room.

"In some way, I find myself pitying the man." Faruq muses. "I have known him for a long time. I think he is a good man, otherwise he would not have come to warn us."

The sky outside the barred window has darkened to a deep blue with hints of black, filling the night sky with mystery and wisdom.

The howling of the wolves has abated. The energy in the room is low. Although tired, I sense that each of us is apprehensive to fall asleep.

I fall into an uneasy slumber. At once, I see myself flying over a moonlit desert, currents of cold and hot air beneath allowing me to rise and fall in an exhilarating fashion.

Suddenly a small hawk is fleeing before me. With absolute certainty I know that this is a spy hawk from Schiraz. I find myself swooping down and with one scream, tear the hawk with sharp claws and beak and watch it fall to the desert sands below. I wake up with a start. I wonder if I have momentarily experienced and seen what Ijlal sees as he checks for messengers leaving or entering the city.

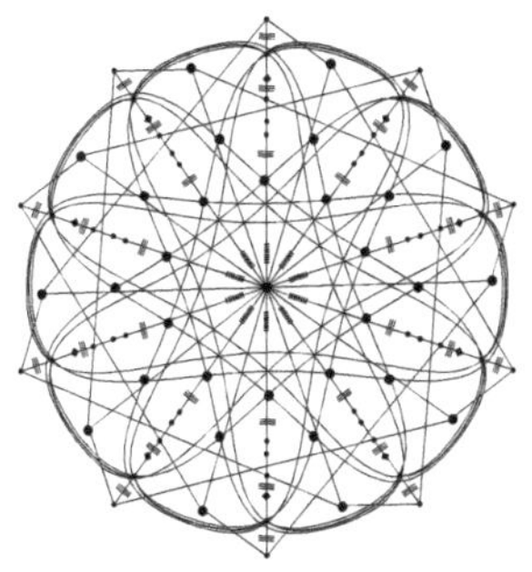

CHAPTER TEN

Wolves howl intermittently all night. Camlac drifts across the sky plunging the room into almost total darkness. I rouse myself from a light slumber and go to the window. The sky has begun to lighten. Looking out, straining to see the northern sky, I can just make out the constellation of the fire beast as it begins to fade in the early dawn.

The voices of the guards outside gradually become more anxious. Their brief tense conversations audible through the wooden door; some even suggesting that they should no longer be standing guard at this post.

"We could tie them up and throw them over the walls and let the wolves finish them." The audacious whispered comment is met with a brief tense silence.

"Do you really want to confront that magician? Did you not see what happened to Vatsarah?" There is no response. "There is no way I want to meddle with such a magician."

I continue to drift in and out of slumber. The soldiers have stopped speaking. The occasional rustle affirming that they are still standing guard.

Unexpectedly, the wolves have stopped howling. An eerie silence drapes the outer walls of the city of Ahvasar. Sudden shouts, followed by hurried footsteps grow louder in the hall leading to our room.

A sharp order is given from someone in command, that they are to take the lower tunnels beneath the outer wall and take to the ships in the harbour.

One of the soldiers calls back, "What of the prisoners?"

The same voice answers roughly, "Leave them!"

We have all heard the exchange. Faruq is standing at the door, his whole-body alert and ready. The twins stand on either side of him.

The soldiers hurried footsteps recede down the hall, the echoes of their hurried exit fading quickly. Faruq tests the door, but the lock is firmly in place.

"Faruq, let me." My voice is calm. Faruq and the twins turn and seeing the light in my eyes, step away as far as the constraints of the room will allow. The fire in my spine rises, only a brief instant passes and the door explodes outwards.

Faruq turn to the twins, "Isamadeen, Rauf, can you lead us to a place where I can see beyond the city walls?"

With a firm nod and decisive steps, the twins lead us through long corridors that twist and turn and eventually lead to a narrow set of stairs. Taking the steps almost two at a time, Faruq rushes up, reaching a platform surrounded by large stone ramparts.

The view of the desert is expansive and takes in the large wooden gate and its battlements at the entrance to the city. The battlements appear deserted, not a single soldier stands on the outer walls. Below us, a large contingent of soldiers led by Captain Eslan is waiting inside the city gate. The captain appears to control his men with some difficulty, moving on horseback from group to group, giving orders and re-establishing order.

On the opposite side of the platform where we stand, there is a clear outlook of the gulf and the two ships at anchor.

My attention is immediately drawn back to the sands outside the city gate. Astonishingly, hundreds of grey wolves have begun to file out in small numbers and disappear quickly into the surrounding dunes.

A small army appears from behind a large dune and takes position in a precise arc made of three sections, cutting off any possible escape into the desert. Anyone attempting to escape between the sections would be cut off immediately. Excitement fills me as I see the royal pennants of Schiraz floating lazily in the early desert breeze. A gold edged triangular canvas featuring a large symbol of the famed ruby of the Schiraz tree, against the royal blue representing the great ocean of Elwah, is fixed to a long pole.

It stands proudly at the fore front of the army. This is the pennant of the Royal Guards–Ijlal's personal army. The young Prince is on his white steed and stands, almost aloof, waiting.

My heart leaps in my chest as I see the large white wolf look up once in our direction, appears to hold my gaze, and deliberately turns and disappears into the surrounding sands.

Saeed is next to me and has obviously seen it as well. "It has held out until Ijlal came." He whispers, awe and gratitude filling his voice.

A single sentry positioned out of sight on the rampart, calls out to captain Eslan, in a strained voice, detailing the army that has cut off the city from the desert.

There is an audible whisper that rushes through the soldiers like a wind through tall grass. Eslan barks out a short command for order. The captain's horse responds to the nervousness, pawing the ground with one hoof.

"They don't stand a chance." Faruq's whispers with a shake of his head.

"Are you speaking of the men below?" I ask.

Faruq gestures to the small army outside the walls, "Those are the Royal guards. Ijlal's personal army. You have seen the companions in action, Azizi. Imagine a hundred of them, that's who these men are." Faruq shakes his head, a crease furrows his brow, contemplating a decision. He steps decisively to the edge of the platform, potentially risking an arrow from one of the trained archers.

"Captain! Why sacrifice your men for the exarch's treachery? There is a better way!"

Eslan pulls his horse to a standstill, looks up fiercely at Faruq.

"I am duty bound to defend this city, general!"

"Captain, who are you defending? Where is the exarch and his followers, including the generals who advised him on this mad course of action?"

Captain Eslan hesitates. Faruq turns briefly to Rauf and Isamadeen, "Quickly look to the harbour, what can you see?"

Isamadeen's keen sight does a reckoning. "I recognise the large stature of our uncle, making his way to the harbour."

Rauf adds sniggering, "I've never seen our uncle move so fast."

Isamadeen turns back to Faruq, "At least a hundred men follow him. I see at least two generals among them. They will board one of the ships very soon."

Faruq turns back to the courtyard below, states in a voice that reaches every man below, "Your exarch is boarding the ships together with his generals and followers. Captain Eslan, you and your men have been abandoned."

There is a stunned silence, and the men begin to stir, the neat columns lose their coherence.

Faruq turns to me, an urgency in his eyes, he whispers, "Azizi, I will go down and reason with Eslan. Would you and Saeed be prepared to call upon the Sacred Tears?"

Saeed and I look at each other and with one accord, nod.

"I hope it won't come to that." Faruq frowns, he releases his breath as his face lights up, "at least we have the power of the Tears with us." He turns once more to the courtyard below and calls out, "Captain, I am coming down. Do not engage with anyone."

As he turns back to the stairs, he hesitates a moment, and with typical directness asks, "Can you or Saeed do anything to delay the ships from leaving the harbour?"

Saeed immediately steps forward, an enigmatic smile on his lips, declares, "I can call the waters of the Ocean Malkizar to stop them."

Faruq stares a moment at Saeed, nods his head once and goes down the stairs to the courtyard.

Saeed steps to the east side of the platform, staring at the harbour and the two ships. The last of the soldiers accompanying the exarch have finished boarding. Commands are carried upon the wind, ordering to weigh the anchors and prepare to set sail.

He looks at me once, his face changing from the boy I have

come to know, to a young adult magician, who suddenly realising the responsibility of his power, hesitates and then taking a deep breath, closing his eyes, asserts his confidence.

"Näcken Malkizar, beto!"

Silence. It is the silence of one measure of time, the time it takes for the sky to roar after a flash of lightning.

My arms are covered with goose bumps. The twins stare at Saeed.

A low rumble at first, followed by a short sudden gust of wind and on the water, the ships begin to dance, slowly at first. Eddies of water begin to boil around the hulls. The ships masts start to sway violently from side to side. Before our eyes, the water in the harbour swells, slowly lifting the ships and pushing them toward the land at the end of the harbour. Yells of the captains, mixed with screams of fear are carried on the strengthening breeze from the ocean Malkizar.

Though the ships are now grounded on the beaches, colossal waves continue to pound the hulls. Laying on their sides, the wooden hulls begin to yield and with loud ear-splitting cracks start to tear apart.

Saeed looks at me, concern in his eyes. I understand that to call the power is one thing, there is also the need to control it and, in this case, call it to stop. Prince Elwah had called the ocean of Elwah to calm the storm of Malkizar. In this case it may not be as effective. I step to Saeed and utter in his ear the words that my intuition has whispered to my mind. It is his power that called the Näcken, it must be his command to control it.

Saeed turns back to the harbour and calls out: "*Näcken Malkizar, Eter-emlak*!"

The effect is immediate. The waves collapse midway through

their assault, the eddies of the harbour merge back with the deeper water, the white angry tips of the waves vanish with the wind and the ocean Malkizar draws itself back to its natural place.

The twins give a collective sigh of relief, their eyes round with admiration.

Saeed turns to me with gratitude and wonder in his eyes. “Thank you Azizi, I will not forget.” He whispers.

“We should go down now and see if Faruq needs us.”

We reach the courtyard. Faruq and captain Eslan are facing each other, an obvious disagreement hangs in the air. As general of the Sultan’s army and cousin to Ijlal, Faruq outranks the captain. It seems that as the only senior officer left in Ahvasar, Eslan wants to stand his ground.

“Captain, I am not against you. You are not my enemy.” Faruq’s firm statement does little to change the captain’s attitude. I sense that if challenged, the soldiers of Ahvasar will side with their captain.

“The sultan’s army stands at our gates, general. Who is to say that they will not make an example of us?”

“This situation is not of your making, Eslan! It is the treachery of the exarch. You will not be held responsible unless you insist on standing your ground and defend his actions.”

“Captain.” Eslan turns to face Isamadeen. “The ship with our uncle and his men have run aground at the far end of the harbour. The ships lie on their sides; waves have smashed their hulls. The exarch has nowhere to go. If nothing else, you and your men should make haste and take them to the Sultan for his judgement.”

Captain Eslan looks uncertain. His eyes move from Isamadeen, to Faruq then me and back again.

"How is that possible?"

"The Sacred Tears of Apphat are here! They are with us!" Rauf asserts in an almost amused tone. He gestures to both Saeed and me.

"If you doubt us," Isamadeen interrupts, "then go to the tower and see for yourself."

Eslan hesitates. Looks up at the tower and back to his men. An awkward silence weighs down on the assembly, the jingling sound of `horses' bits mingles with the squeak of leather. The dust on the ground stirs with the restless horses and men at arms.

"I think the captain requires proof." All eyes turn to me. I look at Saeed who undoubtedly has perceived my thoughts. He and I move to the gate. Half a dozen soldiers immediately take position in front of the gate blocking our way.

I turn to Saeed speaking to his mind, I ask, *"Do you remember the sacred song Ishtar taught us?"* His thoughts affirms that he does. He and I hold both hands at chest level, just below our hearts. Focussed internally, I release all other thoughts and focus on the memory of the song the goddess Ishtar taught us. It does not have to be spoken out loud. The sacred melody comes to me, and I hear Saeed's mind echo the words. The words are strange, they take shape in my mind and manifest in gold letters, similar but more ancient than the runes I studied in my youth.

This is an event spoken of as legend. Not witnessed in a hundred years. The sudden weight of responsibility for manifesting the Sacred Tears of Apphat fills my mind, and the excitement of it makes my heart race loudly in my chest. Fragments of discussions as a young apprentice with my god mother flash through my mind; I hear her kind and serious voice echo, encouraging me to study the legends as told in ancient books. To pay attention to the stories of the Great Creation, how the two oceans were the Tears of the Great Spirit.

The air is suddenly heavy. Its stillness binds, soothes and takes away any sense of resentment, fear, or anger. The soldiers before us begin to tremble, some even falling to the ground. I see reflected in their eyes the power that begins to flow.

A flame emanates around Saeed and me. I witness the Sacred Tear of Malkizar appear, floating above Saeed's cupped hands. The Sacred Tear of Elwah manifests above my hands, glowing the purest blue. The light protects us, spreads outward; it penetrates the very core of each person present.

The twin flames intertwine forming a wall of teal that at once seems to penetrate the very wood of the enormous city gate. The wood creaks loudly and the gate opens as gently as if it had been pushed by a single person.

The air becomes charged with the scent of orange blossoms mixed with the sharp perfume of pine needles after a summer rain. Echoes of words begin to swirl in my mind, *desert spring, fire and ice, moss, and spice, the lock of stone,... at each word, the sky fills with light and then darkens. Clouds swiftly drift past at incredible speed, chased by a silent wind. Day folds into night and folds back into day. The morning fills with birds singing, men shouting, babies crying, mothers laughing; the sound of the desert wind intermingles with the rush of a torrent stream. The Tekbiek bird calls out a sudden and eerie warning, a desert scorpion scuttles beneath the whispering sand.*

SILENCE. A silence so deep that the air itself weighs upon my spirit. The bell of the temple school of Asfaine rings once, singing a harmony more ancient than the sands of the Great Desert of Keyab; my god mother's voice calls out, "*I will name him, Azizi.*"

High in the sky, the crescent moon of Camlac holds out an embrace to the full moon Ayshah, both together in the same sky in a hundred years.

A deep silence fills the courtyard. The world holds its breath.

A clatter of swords, bows and spears shatter the silence as weapons fall to the ground, released by their owners.

The gate is wide opened, I imagine the scene that confronts the royal guards of Schiraz. A young man with hair the colour of a sunset and emerald green eyes, stands holding a large sapphire glowing a deep green, while another slightly older, pale as snow with dark black hair and piercing blue eyes, stands next to him holding a sapphire of purest blue; that scene must be chilling. Every soldier in Ijlal's army, almost dreamlike, lays their weapons down.

Ijlal dismounts his horse and carefully steps towards me. He pauses a moment, his voice testing the sound it makes in the air.

"Azizi?"

"Ijlal, you came quickly. Thank you."

Ijlal looks from me to Saeed and back again. He seems unable to know what to say. Both Saeed and I have released the stones, as they float next to us. The air sparkles around us. Judging by the expression on Ijlal's face and that of his soldiers, it must be an awe-inspiring sight to witness; the Sacred Sapphires enveloping us with its specific hue and spreading outwards. Ijlal hesitates once more then decisively steps and embraces me, and then Saeed, who invariably blushes. The light dissipates, the dry air of the desert around returns to its natural state, a slight fragrance still hangs. The Sacred Sapphires dissolve, my body is filled with the warmth I first experienced when Elwah transmitted the Sacred Tear of Elwah with a kiss, a gentle stream of energy flowing down my spine.

Finally, Ijlal stepping away articulates, "This, is the legend of the Tears of Apphat made manifest! I did not think I would ever witness it in my lifetime." He turns briefly and notes that his soldiers have laid down their arms. Turning back, he gives me a smile that lights up his face. "It is true then. The power of the Sacred Stones inspires harmony, enough that no man wants to fight."

Faruq is beside me, "Cousin, thank you for responding to Azizi's call."

Ijlal briefly embraces Faruq then scanning the soldiers assembled in the courtyard asks, "Where is the traitor Padua? And are these soldiers to challenge us?"

"Cousin, the exarch and his followers boarded their ships hoping to escape by sea. Fortunately, we have the Sacred Tears of Apphat with us. Saeed and Azizi managed to strand the boats at the far end of the harbour. Now that you are here, we can easily take them. Since your army travelled the night, I propose that we take Captain Eslan and his men."

"Can they be trusted? Are these not the same men that held you prisoner earlier?"

"Ijlal, the treachery was the Exarch's and his generals. I have known Eslan for a long time. He was foolish to follow the orders of his superiors, but he is not a traitor to the Sultan."

Ijlal considers Faruq's words, his warm amber eyes searching his cousin's piercing blue eyes; finally nods in agreement.

Ijlal deliberately walks up to Eslan, who salutes him on bended knee.

"Your Highness."

Ijlal cuts quite a figure, dressed in his royal battle gear. Gold breast plate featuring the red flower of Schiraz over a white short sleeved linen gambeson.

"Captain, thank you for your welcome." Captain Eslan looks up briefly wondering whether the remark is genuine or sarcastic. Ijlal gives him one of his most charming smile.

"Captain, will your men follow your orders?"

"Your highness, they are loyal to you and the sultan."

Ijlal nods and gestures for Eslan to stand, "Very well. I understand that the Exarch's boats have been stranded at the far end of the harbour." Eslan gives an astonished look. "Leave enough men here to safeguard the city. You and the rest, join me and my guards and we will apprehend the exarch Padua. I will then bring him to my father for his judgement."

Eslan bows his head and gives the order for his men to follow him and the prince.

CHAPTER ELEVEN

Faruq briefly leans to Prince Ijlal, mutters a few words. Ijlal inclines his head, considers Faruq's comment. and turns to me once more.

"Azizi, my cousin recommends that you accompany us to apprehend the exarch. I do not anticipate much resistance since I have a hundred of my royal guards. In addition, the soldiers here with captain Eslan will be more than enough to apprehend the traitors. I do not wish to impose on you or the Sacred Tears of Apphat. Please let me know what the Great Spirit would advise."

A swell of emotions fills me. Gratitude that the prince of the realm would regard me with such deference, willing to submit himself to the advice that would flow through me. Truly, when Ijlal comes to the crown, I make an internal vow to always serve him to the best of my ability.

"Thank you Ijlal," an old familiar sensation, like snow falling gently around me, a gust of wind whips around bringing tears to my eyes. Suddenly the taste of salt is upon my lips. Ijlal physically steps back, awe written on his face. I see reflected in his eyes, the blue light of my eyes as it grows and sparkles.

"Azizi?" Saeed is next to me. "Azizi? Do you hear it also?" His voice is distant and echoes slightly.

"Hear? Hear what Saeed?" A small child is laughing, almost giggling. I stare into Saeed's eyes and briefly remember the terror of a small boy stung by a desert scorpion. Saeed's body wavers like a desert sarab, seen from a long way distorted in the heat of the desert sands. Suddenly his body vanishes.

I stare into the empty space where Saeed was just a moment ago. A part of me, deep inside my chest feels cold, unexpectedly empty.

Someone is calling out to me, "Azizi?" The sound is far away, calling with urgency in his voice.

I shake my head, bringing my senses back to the desert, I am outside the walled city of Ahvasar. Ijlal is calling my name, concern in his eyes. The twins are beside him, Faruq stands alert, looking in all directions as if expecting an unforeseen attack.

"Azizi?" Ijlal is watching me with concern. "Azizi, what just happened? Where is Saeed?"

My lungs feel empty, I take an abrupt and deep breath. I look around, trying once more to get my bearings.

"Ijlal, I do not know. I heard sounds that don't make sense. I think Saeed could hear them as well. But then... and then he vanished. I do not know where."

An anxious quiet follows.

"Did he learn the farstep you spoke of before? Or did someone take him?" Faruq asks, his voice tense.

"A duwae ago, Saeed did not even have the most basic knowledge of magic, let alone controlling the farstep." I shake my head, not comprehending what has just happened. "Even I do not know the technique. It requires much concentration." A lump is in my throat, a sadness and anguish fill me. Halim's name floats across my thoughts.

Rauf especially looks lost. Isamadeen is frowning.

"Azizi, are you able to call upon your godmother?" Ijlal asks, compassion in his voice.

Something inside me breaks. Tears run down my cheeks; my breath comes in gasps. Ijlal at once steps up and folds me in his arms.

Haltingly I tell him of the night of our escape from Naasée. "I have not been able to connect with her since."

"Cousin," Faruq voice is tense. Ijlal turns to him. "Cousin, let me take Eslan and his men and round up the exarch and the generals."

Ijlal understands the urgency, but I can see the conflict in his eyes. He recognises my dilemma.

"Ijlal, I am sorry. I do not mean to be a burden to you. Following the exarch's betrayal, you have come to free us and re-establish order in this city. This should be your priority. I will attempt to contact Prince Elwah and make my way to the Huda People. I think my godmother is with them."

I can see Ijlal hesitate, caught between his compassion for me and his duty as the prince of the realm.

"Please Ijlal, I am deeply grateful to you. Do what you have to do."

"Ijlal, I will accompany Azizi to the Huda Pass." Rauf's clear and melodic voice lightens the mood around us.

Ijlal smiles gratefully at Rauf, Isamadeen adds, "I will go with them as well. Ijlal, you have enough men to capture our uncle. To see him would only tempt me to punish him myself." Isamadeen's face is hard, a cold light in his eyes. I can only imagine what he would do.

Ijlal chuckles, "I had better spare him from your wrath then. Go and protect Azizi." With that, Ijlal turns to his men with Faruq in his wake. Faruq has already called out orders to Captain Eslan's men, who seem relieved to join forces with the prince and his guards.

The men march past us, some furtively glancing at me; I catch some making the sign against curses, bringing a sad smile to my lips.

Rauf, Isamadeen and I raid the kitchens of Ahvasar and pack some provisions for the road. We make our way to the stables to find our horses rested and still tethered. I hesitate, seeing Saeed's horse and decide to bring it along with us, a desperate hope that we will find him along the way.

Thoughts crowd my mind. *Is it the work of Ahmad or one of his allies in the Council of Elders? Do they have the power to take someone like that? Earlier on, Saeed was asking me if I heard a voice that spoke to his mind. What voice was he hearing?* A heavy knot twists in my stomach, *the dark sorceress and her tribe that had me captured are still at large. I did not have the chance to ask Hasan to deal with them. Perhaps...* the thought is too much; I chase it out of my head. *Then what or who? Is it possible that Master Sahir managed to perform the farstep on his behalf?* A glimpse of hope enters my heart; the horse I ride keeps pace with Rauf and Isamadeen and breaks into a trot; Saeed's horse is tethered to mine. The cliffs of the Huda Pass just discernible on the horizon, begin to glow faintly with the rising sun.

Memories surface of the first time I made my way into the Great Desert of Keyab with Halim. I had stared at the impossible ocean of sand undulating before me; astonished at the warmth of it and the way it trickled between my fingers. How soon I learned to curse it as it made its way into all recesses of my clothes. Halim first instructed me on how to wear the shemagh to protect my face from the harsh sun. Involuntarily I check now that it is secure and will not come off with the wind blowing directly in my face. I gaze into the distance calculating how long it will take to reach the entrance to the Huda Pass.

Isamadeen and Rauf spur their horses to a canter, it takes me a moment to re-adjust my posture to the increasing rhythm of my horse. What seems like an eternity passes as the shadows of our horses shorten before us, and the sun on my back begins to warm unbearably.

A few moments later, Isamadeen raises his hand to call for a stop. Relieved that the pain against my thighs and back will have time to ease, I pull my horse to a stop and almost falling, I dismount as gracefully as I can, knowing that any desert traveller would know me for a beginner.

Rauf and Isamadeen retrieve a series of flexible poles and swiftly assemble them with a large cloth to provide shade while we take a break for the Cârem; the hottest part of the day, which the desert people use to rest, and take refreshments until the air cools down.

Fortunately, we have enough water for us and the horses. Drinking pouches are attached to their muzzles and filled with water. Isamadeen spreads a large cloth on the ground, opens a pack and offers me and Rauf pieces of the flat bread I recognise. The hard cheese he then offers brings a lump to my throat. This is a cheese made from the milk of ewes in the Asfaine mountains.

I clear my throat and distract myself. "How long do you think it will take us to reach the entrance to the Huda pass, Isamadeen?"

Isamadeen glances at his twin. Rauf is focussed on appreciatively chewing a morsel of bread and cheese.

"Just before sunset." Isamadeen resumes his meal.

I think a moment. The sun will be far behind the Huda.

"Will that not make the pass difficult to negotiate? It will be quite dark by then."

Rauf stops chewing for a moment, gives an enigmatic smile to his twin and resumes his meal.

"You are right, Azizi. The passages will become very dark. The last time we went through with you, it was daylight, and the sky was clear. Some of the rock surfaces are made of some minerals that after being exposed to sunlight, even indirect sunlight, will glow for a long time after the sun has set."

I remember the legends of the Huda Pass. The path is a veritable labyrinth and well-guarded. Without a thorough knowledge of the pass, one could be lost and die in it. Only the initiated or those who have a guide are permitted to travel through. Anyone who enters without either is captured or worse, is never heard of again. Permission is not always granted. Worse is being caught unaware when a Cassim blows, the force of the wind in those narrow passages can shred the flesh of a man to his bare bones.

"Will we need to seek permission to enter?" The anxiety in my voice is obvious.

"You remember that Ijlal as the son of the Sultan had permission to enter and leave at will."

I nod, remembering the discussion with their leader when we first attempted to take the pass as a short cut to the Isthmus of Mina. Even Ijlal was hard put to justify himself as a royal escort.

A small lump forms in my throat, as I also remember the young boy Saeed, who called his mother to act as guide for us. She had recognised me, having offered a life debt to me for saving her son. Fariqa led us through, pointing out the safe passages to follow and then had expressed a wish to send her son to me for training when he came of age.

Isamadeen continues, “Since then, the Elders of the Huda People have granted Ijlal and his Companions permanent freedom to enter the Pass at will.”

I am not surprised, given the reputation of the Companions for their compassion and desert skills; Ijlal as their leader and royal prince must have made a favourable impression on the Huda tribe. I lie down, reflecting on those memories. My eyelids feel heavy and with a degree of surrender I slip into a light slumber. A gentle shake of my shoulder stirs me awake, Rauf is smiling, his gentle manner reminds me so much of Halim.

“It is time Azizi, Isamadeen says we should move quickly.”

The sky is still light, though the light is somewhat different and appears tinged with a muddy yellow. I look around quickly rising to stand, notice that the horses are packed and ready. Isamadeen is fretting a little with one of the packs, glances at me.

“Azizi, we should make haste. Everything is packed. We will need to get the horses to a gallop soon, are you ready?”

I nod my head, a little confused I look around and walk to my horse, Rauf is holding out the reins and turning to his own horse, in one fluid movement sits on his mount.

“Why the hurry? Is it past sunset?” My voice sounds tired and muddled.

Isamadeen turns briefly in his saddle, raises his chin toward the sky in the direction of the city of Schiraz. "I am worried that a Cassim is forming." He turns back toward the Huda Pass and adds, "We will need to push the horses into a gallop; if I am right, we can just make it to the entrance and seek shelter in one of the hidden recesses."

I turn to the sky he pointed out. It has darkened in a short time. The air around us is unusually still. Goose bumps erupt along the skin of my arms. Remembering my first experience of the fury of a torrent of desert sand with Halim, I hurry to mount my horse, I fumble but manage to sit awkwardly. No sooner done, Isamadeen, turns the head of his horse and urges it out into a fast canter. I notice that Saeed's horse is not tethered to my horse, Rauf waits until I follow before setting out, urging his mount, and leaving the loose horse to follow. I understand that tethered, the additional horse could slow us down. Relying on the instinct of Saeed's horse to follow the rest of the pack out of danger is the only solution.

My horse sensing the urgency set by Isamadeen, or perhaps like the donkeys of my mountains sensing that danger is looming, breaks out into a gallop. The relentless rhythm, the air snatching at my clothes, focussing on staying calm, I do what I can to lay low on its neck and let its instinct to follow Isamadeen.

The sky continues to darken. In a desperate movement that nearly costs me a fall, I steal a look behind me. Rauf is only a few paces behind me, his head is low on his horse, his eyes totally focussed ahead, his shemagh covering his face does little to hide the seriousness of his manner. He calls out several times, urging his horse to go faster. The sky behind him is darkening the colour of mud. The line of the horizon is blurred beyond recognition. I turn my head back to the front; my body shudders and I urge my horse forward.

And then I hear a deep, low distant howl.

CHAPTER TWELVE

The entrance to the Huda Pass yawns open before us and as Isamadeen predicted, just on sunset.

It seems smaller than I remember, but the brooding power that emanates from its dark looming depth still sends shivers up my spine. The cliffs rise on either side forming a narrow passage that forces us to enter one rider at a time. The silence is gloomy and unnerving. The air is suddenly cool after the desert heat.

Isamadeen does not let up the pace, still urging his horse to a trot. He searches the surfaces of the cliff face. I remember then that he is looking for the secret signs of the Huda People. Signs that mark a safe cavern that will protect us from the rage of the coming storm. Once the Cassim forces its way into the Pass, it will slash anything in its wake.

From time to time and on either side, other narrower passages open that lead away. At those junctions, the main passage widens enough to enable two riders abreast. Isamadeen confidently ignores most of these, but occasionally hesitates before moving on.

A small gust of wind overtakes us and Isamadeen intensifies his efforts. Rauf calls out something, which echoes against the cliffs. Isamadeen pulls his mount to a halt. Rauf points to a sign that was partially obscured by a fold in the rock. Turning the horse with some difficulty, I make my way back to him. Behind the fold in the rock, obscured in shadow, is a dark opening large enough to let a horse through. The secret symbol is clearly marked to one side: a circle with three intersecting lines, signifying that this is the entrance to a safe refuge.

Rauf and I are already inside as Isamadeen rushes in at the last possible moment. The air has suddenly become heavy. Its dryness prickles at my skin. An ear-splitting growl, like thunder echoing before a storm, bursts through the passage. The current of wind and sand combined rushes past the opening of the cave obliterating any light. Suddenly plunged into darkness, I manifest an elf light and check that everyone has made it safely, including Saeed's horse.

Rauf is sitting as far as possible from the entrance, his back to the stone cliff, his hands covering his ears and his eyes closed. I remember, how the first terrifying experience of the Cassim had reduced him to tears. Isamadeen is sitting next to him, an arm around Rauf's shoulders, reassuring him.

The Ahl-Cassim wails for a short while. With an audible smack the air returns to the cave and my ears pop. We stay put a while, remembering Fariqa's original advice of many duwae ago, that any additional flurries of sand capable of causing harm, could still follow.

The sun has set some time ago, turning the narrow passages

into a barely lit labyrinth. Fortunately, the sand is almost white and easy to follow. The dark blue sky above us is a snaking trail of blinking stars. From time to time, the cliff walls seem to sparkle like the stars, blending extraordinarily with the night sky, leaving me with a strange, disoriented sense of walking among the heavens.

I begin to wonder how Isamadeen, who to my knowledge has only been through these passages once, is able to navigate with such confidence. I look up at the stars and realise that the passage we are travelling along must be facing north. With a leap in my heart, I recognise one of the first constellation to appear in the sky; it is the one Saeed, and the desert people refer to as 'Agapé'. My godmother referred to it as the Great Fire Beast, and had pulled out an ancient text, detailing the legend of *The Princess of Balthazar*. A legend of love and sacrifice.

I let out a satisfied breath, knowing that Isamadeen is using the ageless way of navigating at night using the stars as a map.

Following a few twists and turns, the path opens abruptly on to a large sandy clearing. The tops of the cliffs are edged with the silvery light of the moon Ayshah.

I immediately recognise the rocky cliff face. Although seen many duwae ago with prince Ijlal, the sight of it still leaves me awe struck.

The façade of an ancient temple carved out of the solid rock faces us. The elaborate entrance is flanked by mighty columns, each decorated with intricately carved objects and mythological creatures. There is no door, the entrance is open and leads straight into the cool dark heart of the cliff. Imposing beasts carved out of solid rock stand guard on either side, leaving no doubt that to enter this temple with ill intent will be met with fierce consequence.

"Take your possessions and leave the horses here. They will be looked after." Isamadeen's whispered instructions seem loud in the majestic silence of the temple clearing.

Here and there, the passages are lit from deep clefts in the walls that open to the sky, allowing natural light to diffuse along the way. The light bounces off the fine crystals that line the stone walls. From time to time and at certain junctions, the way is lit with burning torches. The atmosphere conveys a sense of calm and quiet.

We come to the end of a long straight passage. Isamadeen comes to a stop and holds his hand to signal for us to stop behind him. I reach him before Rauf; a cavern of immense proportions confronts us. At one end three small men, no taller than Rauf, are standing placidly as if they have been expecting us. One of them steps forward and addressing Isamadeen states, "We have watched you enter the pass at sunset. You did well to avoid the Ahl Cassim. Are you seeking passage or an audience?"

"We seek an audience." Isamadeen quietly affirms.

Although I know that the passages are watched from indiscernible openings in the cliffs, I am still impressed at the covertness and continuous observation of our progress. I can't help but think, *would they have intervened if we had not found shelter, or abandoned us to the ferocity of the Cassim?*

Almost as an answer to my thoughts, the one who spoke turns and addresses me, "Master Azizi, you are welcome and expected. The Companions of prince Ijlal are also honoured and welcomed."

My mind races to know who it is that is expecting us.

"Please," the man gestures for us to follow, "we will take you to the council of Gaisha."

We follow in silence. Their steps on the hard stone ground do not make a sound. A short while later, we are shown through the only set of wooden doors I have seen, into a large well-lit circular room. A memory surfaces from many duwae ago, when prince Ijlal had negotiated with their leader for safe passage through the Huda Pass. This is the Huda People's council room, where all the decisions are made. There are several openings at the other end. My eyes have only just adjusted to the light in the room, when suddenly a figure dressed in the light-coloured clothing of desert tribes, appears at the far end, and runs at me with breath taking speed.

"Azizi!" I am almost knocked over with the impact. Saeed is holding me in a bear like embrace and will not let go. His chin just reaching my shoulder, he keeps repeating my name in between each breath, "Azizi, Azizi." Like an early morning mist, that dissipates with the rising sun, the fragrance of orange blossoms envelops me.

I gently pry myself from his exuberant embrace. His face is beaming, his eyes moist with tears of joy, stare at me with heart-warming devotion. I fold him back into my arms, "Saeed. Saeed, I did not know what had happened to you."

He gives me one of those boyish smiles, asserting "I am here." As if this naïve statement could explain everything. In its simplicity, '*I am here*' is all that is needed.

"Saeed?" Rauf's soft question is immediately answered with a ferocious embrace. Rauf has hardly recovered, that Isamadeen endures the same fate.

"I see that Master Sahir's ward has gained his own tribe."

An elderly woman has entered, looking on with amused enchantment. She has grey hair, standing straight, imbued with an air of authority and calm about her, her deep amber eyes catch every nuance. I recognise her immediately, and in the fashion for greeting important elders, as taught in the temple school of Asfaine, I place my right fist into my left open palm and bow to her, "Greetings Gaisha! It is an honour to meet you again."

She gives a little chuckle, walks up to me and holding both my hands, looks deeply into my eyes, "Young Azizi, you are welcome." Stepping back, she takes a longer look at me adding, "You have grown worthily into your manhood."

I feel myself blush and bow my head.

"We know the reason for your arrival. We planned and coaxed your decision to come here, as time is short." My face must have shown my confusion, Gaisha smiles before adding, "We will explain once you have rested and eaten. The men will show you to quarters where you can refresh and rest. We will call you when you are ready and speak then." Without another word, she turns on her heels and leaves the room.

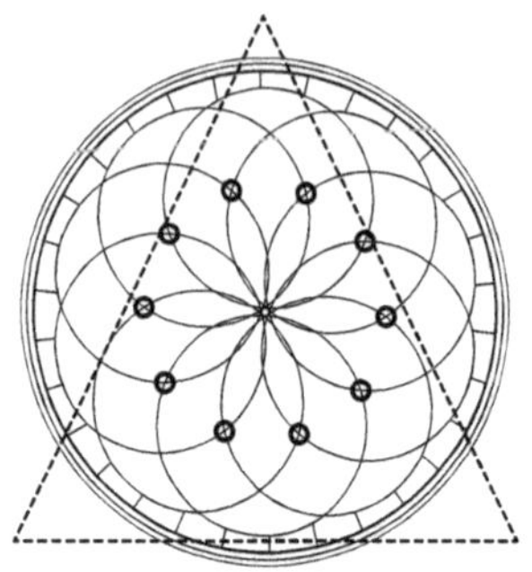

CHAPTER THIRTEEN

I keep staring at Saeed's smiling face.

The others have started walking off with the guides. Absent-mindedly I turn to follow, but then turn once more to stare at Saeed, not quite believing my eyes.

He smiles once more, steps up, takes one furtive look around, raises himself on his toes and lightly places a kiss on my cheek. My senses are again flooded with the scent of orange blossoms. His physical presence undeniable, he smiles mischievously declaring,

"I am not a spirit."

I laugh the comment off.

We reach the designated accommodation and politely and without a word, invited to enter. The room is large, carved out of the rock that makes up the Huda Pass. Low tables are positioned in the centre of the room. They are already laden with wooden plates, glazed clay bowls containing varieties of condiments and small jars some with oils; one heavily decorated I suspect contains a strong wine. The larger ones are filled with water. Large soft cushions surround the table, Saeed leads me to them gesturing to sit next to him.

Looking around the room, a memory surfaces and I recognise that there would be separate sleeping quarters through other openings further down the room. I sit next to Saeed, stare at the food and realise from the sound my stomach is making that I am undeniably hungry. Saeed makes a small giggling noise and piles some flat bread on a wooden plate adding samples of most of the side dishes before handing it to me.

"Saeed, what happened?" I can no longer contain my curiosity.

He looks at me, his face now serious. Looking downcast lost in thought, he looks up. "I am still unsure." He looks back at me briefly before continuing, "I heard a voice call out my name. It was the voice of a man. At first it sounded familiar, but the way he was saying my name was unusual, as if he was speaking a different language."

I look at him inquisitively, "He pronounced it Sah-yed, unlike the way you say it, 'Saheed.'" Saeed pauses. "And then I saw a face, it looked like Master Sahir," Saeed hesitates, "But much younger." Saeed's breathing becomes shallow, his shoulders tense slightly, he turns to me with tears in his eyes, "I recognised the face of my father from the time before he left."

Saeed is quiet for a moment, a tear rolls down his cheek, which he wipes almost impatiently.

"His face disappeared and was replaced by Master Sahir who was calling my name. He bid me look where he was, and I recognised the Elders' council room of the Huda." Saeed's body gives a shudder,

"I was overwhelmed with the wish to see my father and then I found myself here with the Huda people."

Saeed stares at his hands, raising his face to me, tears still caught in his eyelashes, he whispers, "Master Sahir is my uncle." And then almost inaudibly he adds, "My father's older brother."

The sudden news stuns me into silence. I stare at Saeed, slowly making sense of so many things.

"But Saeed, that is good news. You have family now."

He gives me a wry smile. "He used the memory of my father's face to enable me to farstep here."

That also explains Saeed's natural magic ability, it's in his blood. A brief thought of envy twists itself around my heart, *I had to study for mine*. And then as quickly as the thought came, a small voice, that of my godmother assuring my father, *he inherited his mother's gifts.*

"But why? What was the urgency to bring you here?

"To convince you to come in search of Saeed here." Master Sahir's deep and resonant voice cuts through my thoughts. "In spite of my abilities, for some reason I could not contact you directly."

Master Sahir is standing at the entrance to the room, his dark eyes fixed on me. Casually he moves to one of the cushions at the table and sits opposite me.

"I do not know what enchantment protects you Azizi, but it is a powerful one." Quietly he adds, "Your godmother is here with us. I brought her here as soon as Ahmad uttered his cursed spell."

I sit up, my whole attention focussed on his words, The news of my godmother so near fills me with anticipation. "How is she? Can I see her?"

Sahir pauses slightly, "She is still caught in the spell. We have not been able to break it."

Like a stone, the news falls to my stomach and settles there.

"We were hoping that by bringing both Sacred Sapphires, you and Saeed could conjure up a way to break the spell and restore her health."

My throat tightens with my next words, "I thought the binding spell could only be undone by the one who cast it."

Sahir sighs, looks down at his hands and then answers, "You are right. But we feel that the power of the Sacred Tears would be powerful enough to undo that." With a note of sadness tinged with guilt, he adds, "It is unfortunate that the Elders did not see through Ahmad's deceptions earlier." He lets out a long sigh, "As it is, the latest news I received is that Ahmad has been expelled from the Council of Elders and no one knows where he is."

"Master Sahir, can I please see her?"

Sahir looks up, contemplates my question. Finally, he nods his head,

"Yes. Of course. Do not hope too much Azizi. She is still unconscious."

Saeed briefly holds my hand, "I will wait for you here Azizi."

I acknowledge him, grateful for understanding the privacy I desire.

Sahir and I walk silently down several passages and reach a secluded part of the Huda.

Sahir opens a door and ushers me into a large chamber.

The room is bathed with the soft light of oil lamps nestled in niches of the rock walls. There is a bed in the middle of the room. Three women of various ages hover around it, softly repeating incantations. A lump fills my throat as I recognise my god mother's halo like white hair. She is covered with a neutral-coloured sheet. The scent of various herbal concoctions, both acrid and sweet permeate the air. Burning incense leaves a gentle haze around the room. Several powerful rune symbols of protection have been placed around the bed.

Hesitating at first, I step quietly and approach the bed on which Aïschah lies. Her face is relaxed, her eye lids are closed, she appears to be asleep. As I draw near, her lips part as she lets out a sigh. I stop in my tracks hearing my name of power, drawn out with her breath,

"Ah-zi-zi."

Master Sahir looks up at me, a note of surprise written in his eyes.

"She knows you are here. This is the most she has said. It is a good sign," he whispers, a note of hope in his voice.

A murmur of air through the tall pine trees of my forest echoes in my mind.

I relax, like snow falling on grass, my being is filled with the familiar power of the Great Spirit. The women around the bed have ceased their movements. Some looking up step back, awe written on their faces, blue flashes reflected in their eyes.

Images of a mound in the forest, covered with freshly laid moss, a stone carved with runes, star flowers blooming in the shade of tall pine trees, a shaft of sunlight lighting up a name that squeezes my heart and takes my breath away *Halim*; and then more star flowers that somehow float towards me. Suddenly, I am in my godmother's herbarium, a leather-bound parchment opens swiftly before my eyes, remedies written in runes float up. I suddenly realise what I need to do.

"The power of the Sacred Tears will not be sufficient." I hear my words spoken with authority. "I need to collect the Star Flowers from the forest of Asfaine."

I can hear my own heartbeat. Someone slowly releases a breath.

"Azizi, that would mean travelling back to your home." Sahir's words are loaded with doubt. "Importantly, the appearance of those flowers is renowned to be very short. Will their season be over?"

I think back to our recent escape from Naasée. I remember turning to look at the moon Ayshah. It was a thin crescent on the horizon, between the Asfaine mountains and the city of Naasée. I search my memories for the star charts my godmother made me study. I determine that its position indicates that it is late in the season of Malkizar; at least a lahé from when the star flowers will emerge from their long sleep and appear through the receding snow. With a sinking heart, I also realise that I may have missed Saeed's naming day. I push that thought aside and focus on my immediate need to find something that will break the spell on my godmother.

"The Star flowers will emerge shortly. Between the end of Malkizar and the appearance of the new moon of Camlac in the northern sky."

Sahir lets out a long audible sigh. "That does not give you much time. None of us have the skill to find those flowers." His manner is suddenly thoughtful. His eyes drift from Aïschah to me and then back again.

"You have never been taught the 'farstep', have you?"

I shake my head. A small hope enters my heart, that perhaps he will teach me this ability.

"You are reading my thoughts." His words are not spoken in reproach, merely in observation. Sahir nods his head and smiles.

"We should speak somewhere else and leave the healers to weave their spells of protection." As we walk out, Sahir turns to me and casually asks, "Did Aïschah ever teach you to travel with your mind?"

I remember the night she began to teach me this technique, I suppress a smile. The memory of her words of encouragement still echoing in my mind. As I was attempting to follow her instructions, the heat in the room became unbearable. I fell into a trance and began to speak of the Tears of Apphat. Sometime later, Aïschah declared that my visions scared her.

"Yes, Master Sahir, though my first attempt resulted in a deep trance of prophecy."

Sahir slows his pace, stares at me, unconcealed astonishment written over his features.

"How old were you?"

"I had just turned thirteen, Master Sahir." With a gentle pang in my heart, I remember the gift of the sacred gathering knife, with a beautiful handle carved from pear wood.

Sahir shakes his head in quiet consideration, whispers, "so young," and resumes his walk.

We return to our previous room. Saeed is still seated at the table, looking up as I enter, he beams his usual smile that invariably warms my heart. I look around, the twins and Faruq are nowhere to be seen.

Saeed adresses my concern, "They have gone to explore with one of the guides."

Sahir sits opposite us, smiles at Saeed's obvious devotion.

"Saeed, I am about to teach you both the technique of the Farstep."

Saeed's body gives a shudder and incredulously stares at his uncle and then me and back again.

Addressing one of our concerns, Sahir adds, "although neither of you have had formal training in this technique, you, Azizi have had the basics explained to you by your godmother. I think it was her initial intention to develop that skill much earlier than usual." Sahir pauses, with a smile of affection for his nephew he continues, "and you, Saeed, Azizi has begun to train your strength of visualisation. That is why it was so easy for me to initiate the farstep to bring you here."

"Master Sahir," I hesitate, "I thought this technique was not taught until the fifth initiation?"

Sahir nods in acknowledgement, "Yes Azizi. But as I am sure Elwah has previously explained to you, the matter occasionally rests with a trained magician who is willing to instruct an apprentice ahead of time. That is why he gave you permission to train Saeed." Sahir holds up a hand at my next question, "It is also a matter of urgency. Your godmother's condition has not improved since I brought her here." Sahir drops his eyes to the ground, he folds and unfolds his hands, lets out a deep sigh, "We have done everything we can. Her condition is not worse, but it is not improved either. I can sense her fighting to be freed of the curse, but her power is limited." Raising his eyes to me, he adds, "that is why your vision of a cure with the Starflowers needs attempting as soon as we can."

"Uncle?" Saeed's address obviously touches a chord with Sahir who looks fondly at his nephew. "Uncle, how does all this involve me?"

"No one here in the Huda has been to Aïschah's cottage in the mountains. No one here other than Azizi, knows where in the Asfaine mountains the Starflowers grow. Otherwise, it would be a simple matter for one of the trained magicians to farstep and be back quickly." Sensing Saeed's impatience, he adds, "You have experienced the farstep at least twice, once with me as I initiated it at the cave of Gibrar and once at distance with my help and guidance. That alone gives you an advantage." He pauses briefly, "Azizi is trained in visualisation, but he has never initiated the farstep on his own. The farstep needs two specific requirements, first and foremost the ability to visualise in detail your destination and secondly and probably most importantly a strong emotional bond to that place." Seeing Saeed's momentary frown, Sahir admits, "Yes, Saeed. That is why I used your memory of your father's face, that was the strongest emotional bond to the Huda People." After a moment of reflection he acknowledges, "Although the image of your mother Fariqa would have drawn you here as well, your father's image had a stronger pull."

Saeed and I look at each other, a level of comprehension dawning on us.

"The Sacred Tears of Apphat give you both a deeper and more innate power of magic. Using that increased ability, Azizi, your attachment with the Asfaine mountains and your godmother's cottage will draw you there quickly. Returning here, you will need to depend on Saeed's emotional bond to the Huda." The next pause is a little more ponderous, I sense a warning.

"Azizi, sending Saeed with you will give you, a stronger union to achieve the farstep." With an obvious look of affection he adds, "Your connection as Twin Souls will ensure that you will be united in your will to remain together." Hesitating at first, he continues, "The farstep has one serious hazard. While the process when used correctly is almost instantaneous, if during its implementation your mind wanders slightly and you begin to falter in your visualisation of the destination, you could find yourself in a 'mind limbo', a kind of nowhere, which is difficult to undo." With a manner to re-assure us, he quickly adds, "That is why the apprentice is usually accompanied with an advanced magician who ensures a sort of endorsement for a steady mind focus. But in your case, you will rely on each other as twin souls to remain focussed and on course."

I look at Saeed, butterflies take flight in the pit of my stomach. Judging by the tense look on his face, I am sure he is as nervous as I feel.

"Saeed, between us we hold the Sacred Tears of Apphat; are we not the most powerful magicians in the continent of 'Balduh-Shtar'?"

He smiles meekly at me. The tension gets to me, and I start to laugh; it only takes a moment before he starts to giggle uncontrollably.

Sahir shakes his head in amusement. "I will instruct you both later in the day. We should make plans for you to farstep sooner rather than later."

CHAPTER FOURTEEN

Saeed leads me along various corridors, finally arriving at a secluded section that opens up into a large area, the roof of which has a large opening to the sky flooding the space with natural light. Facing us is a medium wooden door heavily carved with intricate decorations of mystical symbols. Saeed decisively steps to the door, presses his fingers in sequence on several prominent features. Following an audible click the door swings slightly ajar.

Master Sahir is already waiting for us, nods in acknowledgement.

The room has been carved out of the solid rock. Its walls are covered in tiny crystal that shimmer with a bright hue that appears to change colour from pure white to pale blues and green. There is a silence in this room that fills it so much that the slightest sound would be swallowed up immediately.

"This is the room that we use for the higher training of those who choose a path of healing and magic." Even Sahir's voice seems hushed, each sound disappearing immediately; no echo to his words follows. "This is where we initiate our students in the technique of the farstep."

The room is devoid of furniture. It appears that instructions here are given solely by word of mouth and physical demonstration. Intuitively, I understand that the techniques taught here are meant to be kept secret. No written records are kept, information is given from master to student along a long line of heritage of such knowledge.

Sahir invites us to stand in front of him and with no other preamble begins his instructions:

"I advise that you do the farstep in two separate stages. A midway point so to speak. Saeed, what do you think about stepping to Madkhal, the village of your Yumma?"

Saeed's face suddenly lights up, a look of unbridled joy at the thought of his grandmother.

"Master Sahir, why two steps and not a direct one?"

"Several reasons Azizi. This will be your first attempt. Although you may be able to communicate to Saeed the image of your destination and the emotion connected with it, for you to sustain the mental image of your godmother's cottage for both of you and over such a long distance is risky. Secondly, on that part of the farstep, Saeed will be stepping with you, following in a sense; the added weight of sustaining the connection for you and him will be strenuous.

So, to make it easier on both of you, the first step of the journey will be to a place that holds a great deal of emotion for Saeed – the village of his Yumma; and on that journey, you will be stepping with him. Likewise, in reverse, the stepping to Madkhal will be easy. The final step to the Huda pass, will be shared between Saeed and me."

I consider his answer, it will certainly be easier and less stressful.

"There is another reason, Azizi." Sahir adds, lowering his voice. "As you may already know, an accomplished magician could easily pick up the trail of magic the farstep uses. I don't need to remind you that you are both wanted by the Elders' Council of Naassée. By breaking up the journey between the two of you, the trail becomes confused and weak and will dissipate a lot more quickly. The identity of Saeed's magic will end at Madkhal with absolutely no trace of your magic. If anyone were to inquire about the whereabouts of Saeed, he would be nowhere to be found in the village, causing even more confusion. Likewise, the magic of your farstep will be different to Saeed's and difficult to track as it begins in the middle of the desert, a great distance from Naasée."

I am reminded of the spell I raised with Saeed to cover our tracks in the sand.

"By the time anyone inquires of your whereabouts in the Asfaine mountains, you will have already left." Sahir lowers his voice even more. "Prince Elwah has been in touch with me. He was concerned for the safety of you both. This is not to be repeated to anyone." Sahir pauses significantly, "Elwah is with Hasan at the Temple School of Asfaine."

My body shudders with both excitement and dread.

"He will ensure your safety, by throwing a shield of invisibility over the entire forest while you search for the starflowers."

I knew Elwah's magic was powerful, but to cover an entire forest...

I release a long sigh of gratitude, both for his aid and the knowledge that he and Hasan are safe. And then with a wicked smile and thought, *I wonder, if mistress Tobba-ha has encountered the prince, let alone the most powerful magician in the land?*

As if answering my question, Sahir states with a grin, "I think Elwah is making himself useful as a talented scribe, by reorganising the library of the temple and annotating some of their more ancient and scared scrolls." With a chuckle he adds, "He may even come across some of his own writings and discourses."

Sahir takes a long breath, appears to bring his internal energies into focus. A moment passes and looking at us, asks, "are you ready?"

A sudden twinge in my stomach threatens to bring up my recent meal. Saeed nods, but pales, accentuating his red curls.

I nod in turn.

"Good." Sahir pauses briefly. "To strengthen your will and to accentuate the magic of the farstep, you both need to focus on the Sacred Tear that you hold. Focus on the place where you know it is held within you."

The green in Saeed's eyes flares up immediately. Equally I note that blue light is reflected back at me from the crystals covering the walls.

"Now, Saeed and Azizi, face each other and hold each other's right hand. Relax. Azizi, slowly focus on the image of your mountain and the cottage of your godmother. Further focus on the strongest and most positive emotion you have for that place. Saeed, allow his mental image to appear in your head"

With little effort, Aïschah's cottage sitting on the edge of tall pine forest manifests in my mind. An urge to run wildly into the forest fills my being. With a strong will I turn back to the cottage. The face of my godmother appears before my eyes, she smiles at me and holding out her hands she offers something. My heart is suddenly filled with anticipation and joy. I sense that I am not alone. Just as the thought occurs to me, I hear master Sahir's voice cut through.

"Azizi, gently come back to this room. Focus on my voice. Sense the air around you and feel Saeed holding your hand."

The room is even quieter than before. I stare at Saeed who is still holding my hand. A look of astonishment fills his features. Taking a breath his voice comes out in a sigh,

"I have never seen such trees. Azizi, they are so green and so tall."

I beam at him, sensing his awe and grateful that at last he has had a glimpse of my beloved forest.

His face still lit up from the experience, Saeed whispers, "Your godmother was about to give you something. What was it that you were filled with such joy for it?"

"It was a gift for my thirteenth naming day."

"Well done, both of you!" Sahir's jovial tone brings us back to the room. "Azizi your image was clear and filled with a strong bond. Saeed, you allowed yourself to receive his mental image and the two of would have disappeared if I had not called you back. Sahir chuckles a little at our dismay. "This was just a test to ensure you were both familiar with the process." He looks proudly at Saeed and adds, "You have done well. Even better than most students I have instructed." Saeed lets go of my hand. Turing to me Sahir remarks, "the instructions of your godmother have stood you well. Your ability to visualise is developed far beyond most students."

Sahir allows himself a sigh of satisfaction. "Azizi, the role will be reversed for the first step. It will be Saeed who will conjure up the image of his Yumma's village and possibly her face. It will be your turn to step with him to that destination. From there, when you are both ready, you will then take the lead as you have just done now and step to the Asfaine mountains."

A mixture of excitement and dread settles mostly in my stomach.

"I will be here again for that first step to guide and as much as possible to follow at least part of the way. I will also be here for your return. Azizi, you know how to mindspeak, I would ask you to use that technique and let me know when you are ready to return."

I stand a little in awe, nod my head and whisper, "Yes master Sahir. I will."

"I suggest that you both rest and come back in the morning."

As we walk out, Saeed reaches out and holds my left hand. He pauses in his step, emotions washing across his face, "Azizi, that was such a beautiful sight. I felt your joy and love for it. I know now why you long so much to be back in your mountains."

I look into his eyes and draw him to me in a gentle embrace. "I am so glad that you could experience that."

"But for our age difference, Azizi, do you think we could have been brothers?" he whispers, an ache in his voice. An ardent look of longing in his eyes and my heart beats more strongly than ever.

"We are twin souls Saeed. Nothing will separate us."

He holds me and I feel our hearts beat as one upon my chest.

CHAPTER FIFTEEN

I skip the early morning meal, remembering the disorientation and sudden movements of the farstep as Aïschah transported me into the cave of Gibrar; uncertain of my ability to keep breakfast down, I determine that I can do without.

Saeed and I make our way back to the training room. Master Sahir is waiting for us, an air of serious determination on his face does little to calm my nerves.

"Azizi, one word of advice, allow Saeed to conjure up the image of his village and of his Yumma. No matter how tempting it might be, resist the notion to anticipate his memory and to add details of your own. Allow yourself to immerse fully in the experience of his memory. It will make it easier for Saeed to then initiate the farstep."

I nod thoughtfully. I have never seen his village and have no concept of it, nor has he ever described it to me. All I know is that his Yumma is loving and kind, and that she loves to wear oil of orange blossoms.

"Repeat the initial steps from yesterday. Face each other. Both of you, focus your energy on the place you hold the Sacred Sapphire. Azizi, hold Saeed's right hand with your right hand, relax and allow your mind to receive the image of his memory."

Small houses made of dried earth crowd together around a well. The image is almost immediate, the impression is familiar and the emotion joyful. Sunlight beams down, dust specks float in the early morning air. The face of an elderly woman crowds my view. She smiles, accentuating years of wrinkles, her eyes are kind, they glimmer with traces of gold that remind me of Saeed's eyes when he was young. Her face lights up, I hear her whisper affectionately, "habibi", which unexpectedly resembles my given name.

I stumble, despite the early morning, the heat of the day over my head is already penetrating. The hot, dry smell of arid sand fills my lungs with a burning sensation. Dazed and slightly confused, Saeed's hand still in mine, I look around and realise that we have arrived not far from the well. An elderly woman with the face I just saw in Saeed's memory is two paces away, at least two heads smaller than him, she stares joyfully at Saeed; calls out,

"Habibi, I dreamed you would come."

Saeed releases my hand and stepping forward, leans down to embrace his grandmother tenderly. I smile at how tall he is that he has to bend. She caresses his face, tears rolling down her parchment like skin, she repeats "Habibi."

The unmistakable scent of orange blossoms fills the air.

He falls excitedly into his tribe's dialect, which reminds me so much of Ijlal's first words in his native tongue. The strange combination of dry whispers of the Nakhla leaves in the wind, mixed with more sonorous sounds of galloping horses on the sand. He gestures towards me as he turns, with a few more excited words, I hear 'Azizi' several times. I understand that he has introduced me to his Yumma.

She steps forward, takes both of my hands in hers, her skin feels cool and surprisingly soft. With the same steely, penetrating look my godmother used when I was a child, she pronounces:

"You are Silver Moon's apprentice. Welcome to my home." The words clear and with a slight accent, she speaks in the dialect of the Asfaine Mountains. 'Silver Moon', is the meaning of Aïschah in the old language. I wonder how my godmother's name is known so far from Asfaine, and intriguingly, how does she know my connection with her?

I can feel my cheeks burn, Saeed suddenly bursts into giggles, one hand covering his mouth, the other pointing at my blushing face; his red curls taking on a life of their own.

I realise that we are now surrounded by children of all ages, whispering, and smiling behind their hands. One of them steps forward and places a hand on my forearm, caressing the pale skin. Surprisingly all of them have much darker skin. Saeed must be the exception in this tribe with his red curls and milk like skin.

His Yumma chases them away and invites us to one of the small houses that surround the well.

The interior is cool, the furniture modest. It reminds me of Ulfa's house when I went to deliver some medicine my godmother had prepared.

Sitting close to Saeed, I lean and whisper, "I do not know what to call your grandmother."

Acknowledging my question, he quickly breaks into his dialect.

His Yumma smiles, nods. She steps over, holds both my hands, looks into my eyes, "Out of respect for your godmother and her healing skills, call me grandmother." She laughs a little and makes a comment in her dialect. I turn to Saeed who smiles broadly,

"She says that now she has two grandsons."

I can feel myself blush. In a low voice I answer, "Thank you." With my right fist in my left open palm, I quickly sketch a bow of respect. and add in a small whisper, "grandmother."

She looks a little astonished but then giggles like a young girl, and adds "You have good manners, Azizi."

It feels suddenly odd to have another 'family' member. Saeed turns to me "you see, we could be brothers." He beams his boyish smile and places an arm around my shoulders.

She nods affectionately, "You are connected. Love and protect each other." A moment later, she brings a tray, with three tall glasses, which she fills from an earthen jug.

"Drink this, it will refresh you."

The drink is surprisingly cool and sweet. I immediately connect the taste, to the oil that Saeed is so fond of wearing. This must be the juice of oranges, diluted with cool water.

Saeed's Yumma is observing me with an intensity that reminds me of Aïschah. She stands up abruptly, speaks a few words to Saeed and leaves.

"Have I done something wrong?" I whisper to Saeed.

Shaking his head, "No. She says she needs to speak to the tribe elder."

A short time later, she reappears with a very old man.

He takes a long look at me and finally nods. He murmurs, "She comes back to us through her child."

Saeed's Yumma holds my hands and with a slight tremor in her voice quietly declares, "You are Caelesti's child!" The old man nods in agreement, smiles once more and leaves quietly.

A knot tightens around my heart.

Saeed looks from his grandmother to me and back again, his mouth agape.

She brushes my cheek lightly with the tips of her fingers, sending a small shiver along my spine. "You have her eyes."

Emotions rise, my throat suddenly tightens.

"I have two daughters. My eldest Caelesti and Fariqa, Saeed's mother." She pauses visibly shaken. "Caelesti married a village chief and left with him for the Asfaine mountains." She catches her breath. "Many years later we heard that she was with child, but that she had died sometime after giving birth." A tear flows down her wrinkled cheek. "For a long time, we did not know what happened to her child. Eventually we had news that Aïschah Silver Moon was raising him as her own."

Saeed now stares openly at his Yumma.

Saeed's breath comes in short bursts, stumbling a little over his words, he asks, "But, Yumma, then...?"

"Yes Habibi, you are cousins. And I truly am a grandmother to you both."

The sudden and unexpected news stuns me into silence. I stare unbelieving and then a crowd of questions flood my mind. *Had I not heard my father call my mother by that name? Why didn't he tell me of my grandmother?* And then an insidious thought, *did master Sahir know and is that why we came here on the way to Asfaine?*

And then I hear a faint echo of advice from my godmother, *listen to your heart, it cannot lie to you.*

I turn to Saeed and look deeply into his eyes, silently ask the question and only my heart answers with a beat as loud as a drum. I then look to her who claims to be my grandmother and see the same answer; her face, though older, bears a resemblance to the painting on my father's desk. Aïschah's voice once more echoes, *you have inherited her magic,* and my father's melancholic voice, *He has her eyes.*

I stand up, my mind suddenly blank, the air laden with the fragrance of orange blossoms, I go to her and gently fold my arms around her, my voice choking with emotions, I murmur, "Grandmother."

The briefest of moments later, Saeed's arms enfold us both. He is quietly sobbing.

"Saeed? Why are you sad?"

"I'm not." In a halting voice he adds, "I am so happy. We have found each other."

CHAPTER SIXTEEN

Saeed slowly releases his embrace, allowing me to face him and see him anew, as my cousin. Pearls of tears still hang on his long eyelashes, his emerald green eyes delve deeply into my soul, his smile still makes my heart sing.

Both of us affirm in unison: "Cousin." I hold him once more, the sense of him even more cherished than before.

The old man re-enters, smiling and without a word, gestures for me to follow him outside.

I shield my eyes from the bright midday sun. No sooner I lower my hand, a high-pitched, trilling sound explodes around me. The entire village is outside grandmother's house. One woman at first trills and she is quickly joined by others. The sound is overwhelming, an intense expression of joy and excitement, my arms are covered in goosebumps.

Saeed and his Yumma are close behind me. Men, women, and

children are all gathered around, smiling, staring, and reaching out to touch my arms, my back, and my head. I am surrounded by a sea of people all welcoming me.

The old man comes over, "You have been raised in the Asfaine mountains. We honour Caelesti's spirit back among us. We have often prayed for her return, she has heard us and sent her only son to us. This is your ancestral home; the people of this village will always welcome you. You have a place among us."

The chorus of the women begins anew, louder and more trilling.

Grandmother holds me by the hand, Saeed places his arm around my shoulder, his demeanour suddenly protective and challenging. I smile inwardly as I notice several girls my age and younger, react with a mild astonishment mixed with a hint of disappointment at Saeed's demeanour.

The old man gestures for us to follow him. The crowd eventually thins out and people go back to their daily chores. We reach a part of the village that is a little set apart, flanked by the foothills that lead to the Asfaine mountains. My heart skips a beat, in the distance I catch a glimpse of a mountain peak etched clearly against a summer blue sky, still covered with a fine layer of snow.

A large grove of healthy fruit trees is clearly visible on the northern side of the village. The trees still bear green leaves. I presume that these are the orange trees that the village relies on for one of their key trade of fruit, but more importantly the distilled perfumed oil of orange blossoms. My godmother's collection of books included some on the production of perfumed oils and their medicinal applications. Other than the calming effect of orange blossom, its more esoteric aspect includes an evocation of purity, and a bridge between the sacred and physical charm. I release a long sigh, in truth, it suits Saeed so well.

The old man stops in front of a large house, steps aside and turns to face us.

"I am Kabir, the sheik," picking up on my frown he explains, "the elder of this village. Welcome to my house." He gestures to follow him.

His house is a little larger than Saeed's Yumma, the furniture a little more refined.

He invites us to sit on some cushions. A woman enters smiling. She is dressed in the fashion of the Tassili, wearing a bejewelled hijab. Her skin a pale golden brown, emphasises her perfect white teeth. She does not speak but her manner is warm and welcoming.

"This is my wife." Kabir briefly introduces us and speaks a few quiet words to her.

I notice that grandmother is sitting very still and quiet. Her eyes mostly focussed on Kabir; she seems alert. I drop my attention to my inner being seeking the reason for her vigilance. Nothing comes to mind, and I determine to stay on my guard.

"Saeed."

Saeed almost jumps at the sound of his name. Kabir is smiling enthusiastically.

"What is it like for you now? To have found your cousin?"

Saeed turns to me, blushing slightly, he reaches out and squeezes my hand.

"I am so happy."

"Azizi?" Kabir hesitates with the name, "That is the name your godmother gave you?"

I nod my head, "Yes."

"It is a dessert name. Unusual for someone of the mountains.

Do you know what it means?"

I can feel my cheeks burn slightly. "Yes. Yes, I do." I think back to the day my godmother chose my name of power and announced it to my father. "It means 'beloved'. It was her special name for me, I was always 'her dear one'". I smile shyly and look at my hands.

Kabir nods in agreement. "Yes, it is a lovely name."

Kabir's wife enters, quietly places some plates of refreshments and a jug of cool drink, and retires without a word.

"Azizi, please excuse my curiosity." I sense my grandmother tense up slightly. I raise my eyes to look at him directly. "We have heard your name spoken with reverence amidst the travelling tribes that come through and trade."

I wait for him to continue. His stare, initially penetrating, now wanders off at my unflinching gaze.

"They say that you are an adept of great magic and that you defeated the evil one."

I don't have to turn to know that the sound of a sharp intake of breath is from my grandmother.

"Rumours are always exaggerated Kabir. You cannot take every story seriously." Grandmother's tone is a little defensive.

"My apologies Aseelah ustaadha. I did not mean to pry." Kabir looks a little put off. I notice that following what I assume to be her name, Kabir adds the title of 'teacher'; it is an acknowledgement of her seniority as a respected elder.

Kabir clears his throat, "but still, Aseelah, his name has been spoken of in the Great Council of Elders in Naasée." Kabir fixes my grandmother with a slightly challenging look.

"Master Kabir," I give him the salute of respect as taught in the school of Asfaine, "I regret to disappoint you." Both Saeed and his

Yumma are holding their breath.

"When I first ventured out into the great desert, I was sent to accompany and protect Prince Ijlal who had come for guidance from my godmother. My godmother, Aïschah had trained me in the healing arts. But she did not teach me the powers of magic as you describe that would allow me to defeat such a powerful sorceress."

Kabir nods his head, initially looking a little disappointed. His gaze changes though. First looking at Saeed who invariably begins to blush and starts to fidget, he turns his scrutiny to me, holds my gaze for a moment before turning to my grandmother.

"Aseelah, it my role and responsibility to protect all the inhabitants of this village. This includes both of your grandsons." Turning back to me, he adds, "Azizi, my welcome to you was given with all sincerity. As much as the village in the Asfaine mountains will hold your childhood heart, you are a part of this village. You will always have a place among us."

I keep my eyes on him, unsure where these assurances are leading. Saeed squeezes my hand slightly, without looking at him I understand that he too is unsure but conveys his support.

"Aseelah, about a mahé ago, two events were reported to me personally that are disturbing." Kabir pauses, "it is known that the exarch of Ahvasar uses falcons to gain information from the surrounding kingdoms. One of our runners found one of those falcons still bearing a message. The bird was dead and had probably strayed or been caught in one of the Cassim."

"The second event came from a travelling merchant. He had taken time to rest at the oasis of Shahreza, whereupon he came across a barely buried corpse of a man, whose throat had clearly been torn by a wild beast. According to the merchant, the tracks left in the sand were unmistakable. They were those of a Fanak."

"Kabir, this is all very disturbing, but what does this have to do with my grandsons." The tone of challenge and protectiveness on the word 'grandsons' is not lost on the sheik.

"The clothes and weapons of the dead man identified him as a known assassin. Deeming the place to be sullied and unholy, the merchant did not tarry long. But before he left, he noticed several tracks in the sand. There had obviously been a struggle. Some of those were those of a caravan that had long gone. The other tracks were of two adults, and strangely those of a Fanak, that either went with them or followed at a distance."

Saeed cannot help but give me a sidelong glance. I squeeze his hand back to reassure him. I sense our grandmother tense up again.

"The merchant followed the tracks for a while. They seemed to be heading for Naasée. Eventually the tracks were erased with the night wind."

Kabir stops again, this time with an obvious intent to emphasise the pause.

"The message from the dead falcon was given to me directly. It was addressed to the Exarch, advising him that two young magicians who had recently left Naasée, were ordered by the Council of Elders to return. An additional note was added that they are to be treated with respect."

The silence that follows hangs like glass.

Yasmin, the sheik's wife re-enters carrying more refreshments.

"Yasmin," Kabir voice is kind but firm. "Yasmin, could you please leave us for a moment?" Yasmin nods and retires.

"Kabir, I do not like the way this conversation is heading. You are drawing all kind of conclusions."

Kabir does not respond, but merely stares at me and then Saeed.

"Azizi, or should I, with all due respect address you as Master Azizi?"

"Stop!" It is quietly spoken, but my grandmother's tone is absolute.

"Aseelah ustaadha, other than the respect I owe you and Master Sahir, Saeed's uncle, I will not let the politics of the Council of Naasée dictate what I should or should not do. Especially if it concerns any member of this village."

Kabir turns back to me once more and is about to speak when my grandmother stands as if to leave.

"Grandmother." Speaking as mildly as possible, I stand and quietly turn to face her.

"Kabir," he raises an eyebrow at the familiarity of my address. "Yes, you may address me as master Azizi." The blood suddenly runs from his face and though seated; he steadies himself.

I turn once more to my kind grandmother; I sense the turmoil and confusion she is feeling.

"We were not meant to stay long. It was master Sahir who advised us to come here first; and I am glad we did. To find a grandmother and a cousin all in one day, fills my heart with joy.

When we left Naassée, under the protection of my godmother and master Sahir, a greedy magician placed a curse on Aïschah. Master Sahir was able to take her and farstep to the Huda." The emotions in me begins to rise again, my throat tightens, my breath is short. Saeed stands and holds my hand. "She is unconscious. She spoke to my mind and under the guidance of the Great Spirit, I found a possible cure. I need to collect some of the Starflowers from the forest in the Asfaine mountains. I need to prepare them according to the lore Aïschah has taught me. I must return to her soon and administer the cure before it is too late."

Aseelah is staring at me. A lump forms in the pit of my stomach. It grieves me that deep down, now, the relationship would change between a newly found grandmother and grandson.

Kabir is speechless and cannot stop gaping at me and Saeed.

"Master Kabir, I can answer all your questions, but time is short, and my godmother is dear to me. She took the place of my mother when my father was stricken with grief at the loss of his wife."

Finally, Kabir takes a breath and concludes.

"Azizi, oh..." correcting himself, "master Azizi."

I raise my hand. "Just Azizi is fine."

He acknowledges me. "I do not know why the Council of Elders want you both to return. I will not obey their edict. You and Saeed are under my protection. I can only imagine that the matter involves magic." He turns to face Aseelah, my grandmother and adds; "You do not have to tell me about this matter unless you wish it and not until you are ready."

There is a knock at the door. Kabir stands and calls out to come in. A young man, obviously one of the village runners, judging by his level of physical fitness, enters, briefly looks at all of us, waiting for Kabir's permission to speak. The sheik nods.

"Master, one of the runners from the north has reported that a large white Fanak has been seen heading through the hills, toward the Asfaine mountains."

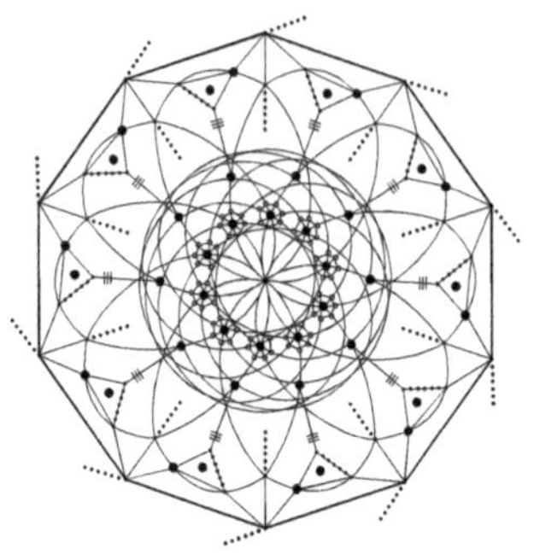

CHAPTER SEVENTEEN

"Summon the hunters."

"No!" Both Saeed and I almost yell in unison.

Kabir looks up in stunned silence. The runner is motionless, shocked at the interjections from the two strangers.

"Master Kabir?" the runner ventures to ask.

"You are not to harm this creature in any way." The authority in my voice, uncalled for, nevertheless triggers the power. The runner staggers back at the light in my eyes.

Saeed's emerald green eyes begin to shimmer. "It is a sacred guardian of Azizi." Saeed declares in as strong a voice as mine.

The runner is fixed to the spot, seemingly unable to move, he stares alternately at Saeed and me. His mouth begins to form words, but he has not the breath to utter them. Unsure, caught between flight or service to his master, he remains awaiting instructions.

"Do nothing Eada. Leave the Fanak unharmed."

Eada barely nods his head, still unable to comprehend what has just transpired, he looks beseechingly at Kabir.

"Do not speak of this to anyone. Go to the kitchen now and ask my wife for a refreshing drink. Thank you for your message. You may leave Eada."

The runner slowly releases the tension in his body, and head down, makes his way to the kitchen.

Kabir releases a long breath. He stares first at me and then Saeed and back again. He begins slowly, cautiously, "As Aïschah's god child, a level of magical power would be understandable. It seems that your reputation does speak truly of your power." He pauses briefly, "But Saeed? I don't understand how that is possible."

"It is in his blood, Kabir. My mother was gifted with the sight. Is it not reasonable that my mother's sister, Fariqa would also have a level of magical blood?"

Kabir stares a while, invariably resting his eyes on our grandmother. Aseelah stares back, not in defiance, but with an air of pride and satisfaction.

With an edge of amusement in her words, she declares, "Kabir, Master Sahir is on the Council of Elders and Magicians. He is Saeed's uncle after all."

Kabir nods his head absentmindedly and takes a step back before sitting back down.

"In fact," I speak the words softy, and affectionately to Saeed, "it was Fariqa who entreated me to train Saeed in the ways of magic."

It is a soft silence, like a landscape after a snowstorm; words dissolve gently into muteness.

Kabir sits contemplating what he suspected and now has been confirmed.

"Not only do I have two grandsons, but I also have two powerful magicians to protect me." Like soft chimes in the breeze, grandmother's words break the silence.

Kabir clears his throat, "Master Azizi,"

"Please, just Azizi. Since I am a grandson of this village, formalities do not apply."

Kabir smiles weakly, nods his head. "Azizi, are you able to tell us what transpired in Naasée?"

Aseelah half stands, reaches out to squeeze my arm. "You do not have to say anything Azizi, and neither does Saeed."

My eyes meet Saeed's and by a wordless mutual agreement, we nod to each other. I take his hand.

"Grandmother," I begin, "It is time that you know of your family's inheritance."

Saeed adds in a soft voice, "It is sacred and something to be guarded against gossip."

We both sit down and face Kabir and our grandmother.

"Master Kabir," I begin, "do you know the legend of the Tears of Apphat?"

Grandmother's eyes open wide and her jaw drops.

"Yes.' He whispers.

"For a long time, the Sacred Sapphires were separated. The Sorceress, using dark magic had managed to force one into her hands and was searching for the other. The result was chaos throughout the land of Balduh-Shtar."

The memories of my godmother's teachings surface, the stories told by the fireplace in the herbarium, her determination that I learn as much as possible, never once hinting that she knew I would play an important role, leaves an empty space in my chest.

Saeed sidles up to me, his shoulder touching mine, he turns to me with an encouraging smile. I take a breath and continue.

"There was a prophesy that the sorceress would attempt to wield her powers and control the world. But the prophesy also spoke of Silver Moon and the power she would wield to defeat the witch – not directly but through the aid of seven companions and a sacred Tear." I take another breath, "this is the dream that Prince Ijlal had come to see Aïschah about." Kabir and grandmother listen awe struck, their attention like young children, drinking the story word for word.

"The story is long, filled with hardship, betrayal and death." I pause, I squeeze my lips together, biting hard to fight the tears brimming at the memory of Halim. Saeed places his arm around my shoulder, strengthening my resolve to keep going.

"I will shorten the story. Prince Elwah, Haafiz of one of the sacred sapphires had been betrayed and captured by the witch. She was hoping to convince the people of Naasée to relinquish the Sacred Tear. Little did she know that it was held within his body.

Tortured and unable to free himself, Elwah did the only thing he could. He materialised his spirit and passed the Sacred Tear of Elwah to me."

Kabir gasps, his eyes round and wide gape at me.

"With the Sacred Tear of Elwah, I was able to defeat the sorceress. She was reduced to a mound of salt where she stood. The prince was released from the spell. Both sapphires were then reclaimed by the goddess Ishtar."

The room is filled with only the sound of my heart in my chest, the soft breathing of Saeed next to me, the rustle of my grandmother's dress as she gently adjusts her posture and leans in, and the release of Kabir's long held breath.

"Recently, prince Elwah advised the Council of Elders that the time to recall the Sacred Sapphires had come. According to prophesy, he claimed that twins had been made manifest in the world, who would take charge of the Sacred Twin Sapphires. When questioned, it was affirmed by one of the elders as well as master Sahir, that the twins, are..." I look deeply into Saeed's eyes, "Us." We both intone at the same time.

"That is not possible." Kabir shakes his head in disbelief.

"We are not twins by birth, that is true." I state.

"We are Twin Souls." Saeed finishes.

Tears are coursing down our grandmother's face. Her voice shakes a little as she speaks, "I know this to be true. I have dreamed it many times but could never understand the meaning of seeing Saeed and another boy next to him, until I laid eyes on you Azizi."

"Following the ritual, we each chose one of the Sacred Sapphires. Malkizar is within Saeed, and Elwah is within me."

The silence is broken with a muffled sob from my grandmother, she stares at both of us and opens her arms, inviting an embrace. Saeed beats me to it, but gently I position myself next to him to receive her hug.

"Are you saying..." Kabir's voice is subdued and hesitant, "are you saying that right now, in this room, in this village, both of the Sacred Tears of Apphat are present?"

"Yes, Kabir." Both Saeed and I affirm.

"Master Kabir," my voice is serious. He looks up, more than a hint of meekness in his gaze. "It is important that what we have told you remains a secret. There is greed and confusion in the world, not less among the magicians of Naasée. Prince Elwah was forced to resign both his role as Haafiz and regent ruler of Naasée. Elwah knew that if the Sacred Tears of Apphat were handed to one of the elders, it would tear the Council apart and would result in another war. They questioned his authority, and so he resigned his position and title.

The magician that cursed my grandmother is one of the elders who refused to acknowledge his choice of Saeed and me as Sacred Keepers. That is the reason my godmother and Master Sahir had chosen to take us away from Naasée and hide us."

Kabir slowly signals his willingness.

Suddenly Saeed's hands fly to the sides of his head, his legs give way, and he lets out a yelp of pain.

I quickly catch him before his head hits the stone floor. "Saeed, what is happening?"

"It's my uncle Sahir. He urges you to please hurry with the cure."

I stand up, but my knees almost give way. We have stayed too long.

"We must hurry Saeed. Please stand with me and hold my hand."

Saeed hesitates. I frown at him, wondering why he is pulling back from me.

"I will only get in the way Azizi. You know your forest best. I will remain here and wait for your return."

But this is his emotional anchor. How will I return here? We were meant to step together.

Saeed reads my mind. "You have me and your grandmother here now. This will be your emotional bond." He smiles his beautiful boyish smile, "Go now, Azizi."

My mind begins to shape the image of my godmother's cottage, the edge of the forest, the moss beneath the trees...

A fierce wind is blowing. *A snowstorm!* My mind wonders how I could detect a snowstorm from within the farstep. A small fear enters my mind *how will I find my way if the snow is so thick?* An echo of Sahir's warning surfaces: *'do not let your mind lose focus.'*

A young man, skin as pale as snow, raven black hair, penetrating blue eyes is sitting in the middle of a snow field. Rays of pure blue light spread all around him. He looks up at me and smiles, a simple but comforting smile.

"Who are you?" I ask

"I have been waiting for you for so long, Beloved."

I can feel my face turn into an inquisitive frown. The voice resonates with tenderness. An overwhelming energy of love emanates from him.

I whisper once more, "Who are you?"

In the gentlest tones the being of light answers, "I am the most sacred and unique part of you, I am the best and most exquisite essence of who you are."

Light fills the space around me, it penetrates me, it surrounds me and somehow it fills every part of my inner being. An overwhelming sense of love fills my chest; my mind, my entire body resonates with this energy.

"Remember to hold his hand tight." The voice continues. "He is your mirror. He is your twin. Do not let go, he is the Sacred Keeper of the other side of the bridge."

"Saeed!" I call out suddenly, a small fear to be alone unsettles me briefly.

"I am here, Azizi." Saeed's face is next to mine. The emerald green of his eyes fills me with a longing for the green moss of my mountain forest. The image of my beloved forest and my godmother's cottage on its slopes reasserts itself. The air shimmers, the view clears.

CHAPTER EIGHTEEN

The scent of decaying leaves, the pungent earthy and woody notes overlayed with the sweetness of the pine trees, is the first thing that assaults my senses. My heart at once beats in recognition of my beloved forest, my head is dizzy. One knee on the damp earth, my hands hold my head, trying to overcome the sense of nausea from the farstep.

Unsteadily, I stand up and take the deepest breath I have taken in a long time. The cool forest smell fills my lungs, and it almost hurts after the harsh desert heat. Steadying myself I look around to take my bearings.

With a surge of joy, I recognise the hedge of ferns that lead up into the forest and to a remembered large clearing. Turning on my heels, I recall that the same hedge runs down the hill and will lead to my godmother's cottage.

I turn back toward the dark and damp mystery of the forest.

Beams of sunlight pierce through the canopy highlighting rocky outcrops covered with moss. I step out with determination and reverence amongst the trees. A movement catches my eyes. A bird lands near me mimicking the bird in my youth. Instinctually I reach for one of my pockets hoping to find breadcrumbs. As I draw my hand out, I am astonished that it flies up to my hand to examine the content.

A squirrel scampers up a tree, makes a quick chattering sound and disappears into the upper branches.

A voice calls out, "The forest likes you, young Master." I jump at the words, my heart skips another beat, the words echoing those of Halim so many duwae ago. My sudden movement scares the bird off.

I turn to see a young shepherd roughly the same age as me.

A gust of wind picks up a flourish of leaves and petals from nearby trees, creating a short whirlwind around me.

"You have been away for so long; the forest welcomes you back master Azizi. It dances around you."

I laugh, stretching my hands to touch the dancing leaves.

"What is your name? Your face looks familiar."

"I am called Harun."

The way the Hills People introduce their names, always implies that the name has a meaning. I scan back through my godmother's book of names.

"You are 'high mountain'?"

Harun smiles the same way Halim did all those duwae ago. An expression of pure delight and welcome.

"Thank you master that is right. Though in my case it means '*from* the high mountain."

I nod, trying to remember where I have seen him. As if reading my mind, he states:

"I am cousin to Halim."

The name almost stabs me and my breath catches.

My face must have given my feelings away.

"Mistress Aïschah and you favoured him greatly. I know that he loved and admired you." The pain of hearing him speak in the past, makes my stomach twist again. He pauses reflecting, "Your magic healed his mother when she was ill." Another pause as he looks to the ground and shuffles slightly. "Your healing arts were greatly missed the last duwae." He hesitates, looking askance, "when Halim guided you to the Great Sands and you defeated the evil one..." He looks deeply into my eyes, a question that has been with him for decades, lies unanswered. I would not know where to begin. "Mistress Aïschah followed you sometime later. She brought Halim's body back to his mother's village. Ulfa nearly went mad with grief. Halim was her only son, the only one in the family to sustain her." His eyes momentarily take on an accusatory tone. "The mistress had to leave again, and she has not been seen since. Will she be back soon, Master?"

There again, the title that separates me.

I look down momentarily, brace myself for the declaration I am about to make. I raise my eyes to meet his and declare: "I loved Halim deeply." My throat tightens, my words come out as whispers, "I thought he had safely returned from the desert."

"He had master Azizi. He returned to tend his sheep as he always did."

"But how is it that he was..." The words choke in my throat.

"My cousin loved the mountains. He was skilful at finding new pastures for his sheep." Harun pauses. His eyes wander around the forest, he struggles to find the words to continue. "Shortly after he had returned, his sheep were left wandering the mountain side. We could not find him. Fearing that he had been taken by a wolf,"

Impossible! I think. *Halim fought a Shadow with nothing more than his staff!*

"We searched for him. He used to have a favourite spot on a rock, where he could oversee his sheep and keep an eye on the forest for wolves. He used to play his flute to the sheep. I think they liked it, they never stranded far from him." Harun smiles at the memory of his cousin. Remembering something, he searches a pocket inside the sheep skin covering his torso.

"There were signs of a struggle and we found this." He pulls out a pendant. My heart squeezes in my chest, my knees suddenly feel weak. It is the sacred pendant Aïschah had given him before leaving. A charm of protection.

"I had seen this around his neck. He wore it every day." Arum extends his hand, meaning for me to take it. "I know it was a gift from the mistress. He took such care of it."

"Keep it Harun. It belongs to you; I am sure Halim would want you to have it."

"Master Azizi, do you know what happened?" I take a deep breath, calling upon my teachings to stay in control of my emotions.

"I think the Shadows that worked for the sorceress managed to overcome Halim and take him. I am certain that he fought them off, but in the struggle, the pendant came loose." With a note of melancholy I add, "It was a charm of protection."

Harun nods his head, closes his fingers around the pendant,

briefly brings it to his lips, murmurs a few words in his dialect and carefully places it back in the inside pocket of his sheep skin shirt.

Tears roll down my face, unashamedly, "When I saw him at the hands of the murderous red robe, my world shattered. I am truly sorry Harun, that I could not save him."

I hesitate to ask. "Harun, where did his mother bury him?"

He nods a few times, his brows knit a moment. He turns his head slightly towards the hills and turns back to look at me.

"It was the mistress that took care of that. She took him to a hill where he used to graze his sheep. She raised a mound and a stone over his body and placed strong magic around it, that no beast would ever touch the grave." The emotion catches him by surprise. He quickly wipes away a tear. He looks up, a fierce expression on his face, "No one dares go near it, especially on the full moon of Ayshah. It is rumoured that a fierce spirit guards that place."

My arms are covered with goose bumps. I can vow that the magic Aïschah would have used would last for a very long time. I make a vow to visit Halim's grave before I return.

"Harun, my godmother is very ill. I need to find the starflowers to make a cure. Have you seen any lately?"

My sudden news catches him by surprise, he hesitates, turns his head from side to side, scratches the side of his temple and finally declares, "I think that most are already fading, master Azizi. But perhaps near the tallest pine trees toward the village, there may be some left in bloom."

"Thank you, Harun." Without waiting for a reply, I start to run in that direction he indicated.

I reach the tall trees. A vague memory tugs at my heart. This was where I first saw the lady of the forest and the carpet of starflowers in bloom out of season. I stare in disbelief, the grass is wet with dew, not a flower in sight. My heart sinks, my stomach gives a wrenching twist and sweat begins to form on my forehead. *Am I too late?*

"Aldrick?" The softest most gentle voice murmurs my name.

A whisper comes straight from my heart, and I call back, "Mother?"

She beams her wondrous smile, like the picture on my father's desk.

I look at her shimmering form, my voice near breaking point, "Aïschah is very ill. I need the starflowers to make a remedy. Please mother" I implore, "can you please call them back from their slumber like you did once for me?"

She smiles a kind but melancholic smile and quietly states, "You will not need them Aldrick. Aïschah is returning home."

I stand fixed to the ground for a moment, and without further thought I turn and run through the trees, down the hill, and toward the village and my godmother's cottage. My heart thumping with excitement.

The evening goddess has draped the sky with her robe of dark Tassili blue, adorned with a thousand scintillating gems. The constellation of the Great Fire beast bright and clearly visible. The second moon Ayshah lies low on the horizon, her crescent shape facing the north star as if ready to catch it.

I reach the edge of the forest. Aïschah's cottage stands outlined in the early evening light. All the villagers are indoors. Plumes of woodfire smoke rise into the cold evening air.

A cold breeze is blowing from the North. Soon the snows will begin to fall. A shiver shakes my body. I force myself to steady my pace.

The warm light of oil lamps and fireplace shine through the closed windows, a sharp contrast to the surrounding cool landscape. I wonder if she has scried my arrival.

I pause briefly, savouring every moment of my arrival, aware of the swarm of butterflies that have taken flight in the pit of my being.

Making my way to the recognisable back door, a flood of memories halts me in my tracks. The old wooden door painted a dark green faces the forest. I remember the day Halim and I rushed in to partake in the feast of my thirteenth naming day. The memory of Halim pulls at my heart, a gentle sad note in another wise happy song.

Gently, I open the door and walk into the kitchen.

She is standing at the stove, watching over a steaming pot. Turning towards me, without a single note of surprise, she looks directly at me. For a moment I think she does not recognise me but then she smiles broadly at me. I stand before her, neither embracing her, nor receding from her touch. I am before her, no longer a boy but a man, an initiate and Seer of Apphat, Sacred Haafiz of Elwah, Tear of Apphat. She steps forward and gently brushes my cheek. The nearness of her touch sending a shiver down my spine.

"You are grown so tall." I hear her whisper.

The fragrance of fresh herbs permeates the air.

First her hand becomes translucent then her whole presence shimmers, fades, and like a mountain mist, gradually dissolves at the first ray of sunlight.

"Godmother," is all I can whisper, and I try to hold back my tears at the flood of memories. And then it hits me, the words of the lady of the Forest: *she has come home.*

Something within me is torn apart. My heart cries the words I cannot utter, *I thought we would live out our days together. I wanted to sit by the fire and listen to your teachings and wisdom. I never thought I would outlive you. You were always guiding me, always encouraging me when I needed you.*

My heart screams, *I need you now!*

The sound of a gentle breeze through the pine trees blows in through the open door and around the kitchen. The fire has gone out, there is no lamp oil lit to welcome me, the room is dark, a silver ray of moonlight cuts across the kitchen table. The sound of the mountain wind stirring through the forest outside is accompanied by a familiar voice, *"My Dear One, I have not gone away. I am always here when you need me. I do not have the power of the magical stone that is within you, which will bless you with very long years. But know this, life will come looking for you one day and invite you to step out of your mortal shell. I will be there to welcome you."*

A long lamenting howl pierces the silence of the night.

I step out and see the white wolf give voice to my heart.

I watch as it howls, once more celebrating the life of the Lady of the Forest, and then turns and disappears into the shadows of the trees.

Saeed materialises suddenly. As soon as he makes eye contact with me, he runs, throws his arms around me, tears flowing down his face, "I am sorry Azizi. They could not do anything to save her. She left whispering your name."

I already knew.

I had just said my goodbyes. My body lies lifeless and limp in Saeed's arms.

EPILOGUE

Many moons rise and sink below the horizon.

Snow covers the mountains and spring comes and goes.

Each season of Malkizar, the lamenting howls of a wolf are heard.

One season, I hear the forest call me. The call is unmistakeable.

I step out of the door of my godmother's kitchen.

The one that opens onto the forest.

The one that had welcomed Halim on my thirteenth naming day.

The moon is high and full, highlighting the pine trees. The forest is solemn and silent.

Out of the shadow of the forest, like a ghost made flesh, the white wolf slowly appears and sits at the very edge.

His piercing blue eyes steadily gaze at me.

Then slowly, he turns his head. As he does so, another shadow slips from behind the trees. A magnificent grey she-wolf. She sits next to him and looks at me with her silver eyes.

They sit there for a moment. The she-wolf turns slightly back to the forest and in between them, three pups slip and sit.

My heart swells with joy and pride to see them. Two of the pups are silver-grey, and one is a pure white, with piercing blue eyes. It rests next to its father.

I hear his thoughts then, *we will hunt most preys in the forest, for we must live. But this I promise, none of my tribe will ever harm any sheep of Halim's tribe. Those will always be safe.*

A moment more, and they turn and disappear into the shadows of the forest.

I am left with an ache in my heart. I do not know if I will ever see them again.

But this is how the legend of the White Wolf of the Asfaine Mountains began.

And true to his words, the sheep of Halim's family were never harmed. Every year, a white wolf appears at the edge of the forest as if it is making a renewal of the vow his ancestor made so many years ago.

On a hill, not far from the edge of the forest, where Halim grazed his sheep, there is a small mound of earth on which moss has grown. Every year at the end of the season of Malkizar, a white wolf appears at the height of the full moon. It gives one long wail and then disappears back into the forest. The following morning a carpet of Star flowers blooms upon that mound. There is a stone that has been carved. It bears ancient runes that best translate as:

Halim, Shepherd, Immortal Beloved
To Azizi, seer and prophet of Apphat.

THE END

DICTIONARY OF NAMES AND TERMS

Aldrik Azizi's child's name. Made up of two parts: ALD/ADAL Norse for 'noble' or 'kind'; and RIK, Old Germanic for 'mighty'. Born on the second hour of the second day of the second month of Winter–A Child of Stardust. Pale, slight of build. Ice blue eyes. Holder of magic. Often misconstrued as 'distant', 'aloof...'

Ahl-Cassim The breath of God, the precursor to the great desert sandstorms the Cassim.

Apphat (pronounced *ap-fat*). Apphat the Wise. Ancient king of Naassée who founded a philosophy based on Androgyny. His philosophy was that the duality of creation existed in both men and women. The Apphatians were known for its fierce, honoured, respected, and feared soldiers.
The kingdom of Apphat was destroyed in the great cataclysm and its people disappeared. Many hundreds of years later, a strange people emerged from the Caves of Gibrar wearing arm bands and amulets that the Apphatians had been known to wear. This people settled in the east of the land and became known as the Naasséenes. They practiced the rites of Apphat. (Refer to *'Apphat The Wise'*).

Aïschah (pronounced *a-ee-sha*) In the Ancient tongue means 'Silver Moon' (see also Ayshah). God mother of Aldrick / Azizi. Seeress Magician, Teacher and Healer. Mahjira or female master of the seventh rite. She lives in the Asfaine mountains and honoured friend and guardian of the Hills People.

Aqueel Young soldier of Naasée. His name means knowledgeable.

Aseelah ustaadha Saeed's Yumma / grandmother. Meaning one who belongs to a great heritage or family. 'Ustaadha' means teacher.

Ayshah (pronounced *a-ee-shü-ha)* The second moon of this world is smaller and has a silvery appearance. According to legend, this moon can overpower the ill omen of Camlac especially if it eclipses the latter during the season of Malkizar.

Ahl-Cassim Literally translated to mean "The Breath of God". A dangerous wind that blows unpredictably through the Huda pass. It can shred a man or beast to pieces.

Ahmad An elder of the Council of Magicians of Naassée. Master of Divinations and Symbols

Azizi Name of power given to Aldrik (Dear One), by his god mother. It means beloved. Named Aldrik, he was born on the second hour of the second day of the second month of Winter—the season of Malkizar, the coldest season of the Asfaine calendar. Also associated with sorrow, the tempestuous ocean that is most fierce also takes on the same name. One of the Sacred Sapphires also takes its name.

Balduh-Shtar The continent that is made up of the Northern regions, the Asfaine Mountains, the Princedom of Naasée, the Kingdom of Glesskerel, The Great Desert of Keyab, the Kingdom of Schiraz, the isthmus of Mina and the Great Citadel and the Huda Pass.

Camlac Name of the first moon of this world. It usually appears first in the cycle of moons, and is usually a pale yellow in appearance. Depending on the season, it usually is taken as a bad omen. It was named after the demi-god its name meaning 'chaos'.

Cârem A desert expression, meaning the hottest part of the day when travellers will rest, take refreshment and possibly sleep until the sun sets and then travel at night.

Cassim A great desert sand storm.

Damna Apphasian for "Sacred Initiation"

Delena Tobaha One of the senior female teachers at the Temple School of Asfaine.

Duna Equivalent to one day, or the time that it takes for the wind to re-sculpt a sand dune in the great desert.

Duwae Equivalent to a year.

Eada A runner from the village of Madkhal – Saeed's grand-mother's village.

Elwah The season of Joy, associated with re-birth and reincarnation. Also the name of the Prince Guardian of the Sacred sapphire by the same name.

Elwah Tahir Official title of the prince: Lord Elwah, Custodian Elwah Prince of Naasée Haafiz (Sacred Keeper) of the Sacred Tear of Apphat for the People of Naasée.

Esai Young household servant to the Exarch in the walled city of Ahvasar. His name means: 'Gift' or 'Salvation'.

Fanak Albino desert wolf. Striking blue eyes and pointy ears able to detect the faintest sound in the desert.

Fariqa Meaning 'Woman Companion.' Mother of Saeed.

Faruq (pronounced fa-rook) Captain of Prince Ijlal's royal army. One of the Companions, meaning 'One who distinguishes truth from falsehood', eldest son of General Giafar.

Farstep The Magician's advanced ability to physically relocate to any desired location. A complex and potentially dangerous technique taught at the fifth initiation.

Glesskerel Kingdom of the Northern Region and country of origin of Shahulm. The nation is situated far north of the

Asfaine Mountains and is separated from the Asfaine on its southern most border by a large glacial wilderness.

Gaisha Title of respect meaning "Great Mother/Father" (depending on gender).

Giafar Younger brother of the Sultan Rashãd of Schiraz, his most trusted general, advisor and uncle to Ijlal.

Gibrar Foreboding and desolate cave legendary place thought to be the last stand of Princess Baltazar and her lover. Renowned for the strange beasts that inhabit the surrounding lands. Used as test of bravery by early Apphat soldiers, also thought to be the place of origin of the Naasséenes.

Haafiz Sacred Keeper

Haakon Aldrik's father. His name in old Norse means high son or descendant.

Hadid One of the twelve ancient guardian spirits. Hadid is the guardian of the air taking the form of a great bird; he is also the messenger of the sun god.

Hala Aura or energy field. Visible to those with the Sight.

Halim Meaning 'gentle'. Shepherd boy of the Hills People. Destined to befriend Azizi.

Harun Cousin to Halim.

Hasan Meaning 'handsome'. Naasseene soldier, Captain of the Royal Guard and personal protector of Elwah, regent prince of the Naasséenes. His official title in Naasée is 'Excellency'. His role encompasses the administration of the city in the absence of Elwah.

Huda Literally meaning conduit, interpreted as Great Mouth. This pass acts as a channel for fierce winds, known as the Ahl-Cassim.

Ijlal Heir and prince to the Kingdom of Schiraz. The leader of the Band of desert youths, trusted for his courage and fierce fighting skills.

Isamadeen (pronounced isa-ma-deen) meaning 'to guard'. One of the Companions twin brother to Rauf.

Ismuth of Mina The narrow strip of land extending from the Great Marshes to the old Citadel, ruled by the Overlord before his demise.

Ishtar Goddess, Custodian of the Sacred Tears.

Jamal Meaning 'kind'. One of the companions.

Kabir Sheik of the village Madkhal at the foot of the Asfaine Hills.

Kershel Measure of distance approximately equivalent to a metre and a half.

Luam Young kitchen hand in Naasée. His name means 'calm'.

Mahjir (pronounced *ma-here*) for a man; **Mahjira** (pronounced *ma-heera*) for a woman. Term of great respect, literally means 'Master' and is given to one who has mastered the arts of magic and seership.

Mahjir (male) **Mahjira** (female)

Mahjir Sahir Mage for the Huda People, member of the Council of Naasée and uncle to Saeed.

Mina Ahmad Master of Divination and Symbols, elder of Naasée. Nasty man. Divination means that he is responsible for interpreting prophesies and signs. He should technically be an expert in astrology and runic symbols.

Mahjir Suffrah One of the revered Elders and Magician. Mater of Rites and Ceremonies. He is the master who initiates Azizi into the First Order of Apphat the Healer.

Mahjira Mitra One of two women and Elder of the Council of Naasée. High Priestess, power over the Summoning of the Guardians.

Malkizar The coldest and most turbulent season of the

Country. The season of Malkizar sees the Asfaine region covered in snow and cut off from the rest of the country for about 3 to 4 months. In our culture—it would be known as the winter of the long night.

Mina The 3 stone pillars. The isthmus of Mina that leads to the stronghold of the Over lord—the great citadel.

Naasée A strange and enigmatic city built on the cliffs overlooking the Great Ocean of Elwah, its people known as both the Naasséenes as well as the old Apphasians. According to legend the people of Naassée emerged from a deep cave following the great cataclysm that destroyed the kingdom of Apphat. They wore the same clothes and talismans as the traditional Apphasians. They are ruled by priests of great magical power; their leader is Prince Elwah. It is said that he is a reincarnation of unbroken lineage of such individuals and is identified by the priests as one of fair skin and blue eyes. Naassée is also known for its fearsome army of unconquered ruthless soldiers, who follow the ancient rites and lore of Apphat.

Nakhla Name of the native tree that grows in the desert around an oasis.

Narn (pronounced '*narun*') Fire.

Noor Light. The name for light is invoked to create an elf like light.

Parvus Sacred rhyming verse written in groups of five lines, mostly used for epic poems and sacred text.

Saeed Meaning 'Happy; Lucky'. Son of Fariqa.

Sahir Young magician (at least 100 years old) on the Council of Elders. His specialty – names and potions. One of the few masters from the Great Desert of Keyab, Mage of the Huda people.

Sarab Mirage - a common phenomenon that occurrs at certain times of the day as the heat from the land plays with images of object or water that are far away but appear to be close.

Shahulm Prince of Glesskerel, named after the Guardian of the Night, meaning Lord of Dreams/Hope.

Shemagh A triangular piece of cloth that is used to wrap around the head and face to protect it from the harsh desert heat as well as cover and protect the mouth from dust and sand.

Tabrass Servant to Master Ahmad. His name signifies 'untrustworthy' or 'liar' in some desert dialect.

Tekbiek Predatory bird rarely seen. Dark in plumage it is adept at camouflage. Amongst the simple folk it is associated with the dark spirits that are said to roam the forest at night.

The Giant's Footsteps A group of large stone pillars so

called as they appear to be steps. Thought to be remnants of formations like the Huda, which have disintegrated over hundreds of years. They are found on the southern tip of the Asfaine Mountains extending across to the coastline southeast of Glesskerel.

Yasmin Wife of Kabir, Sheik of the village

EXPRESSIONS OF TIME

Duna Equivalent to one day, or the time that it takes for the wind to re-sculpt a sand dune in the great desert.

Dahé Equivalent to a day

Lahé Equivalent to a week.

Mahé Equivalent to one month

Duwae Equivalent to a year.

Ulfa Meaning 'she wolf.' Mother of Halim.

Varye Sacred moral duties/codes that bind the magician to using certain powers or techniques only under specific circumstances.

THE COMPANIONS

Ijlal (pronounced *eej-lal*)

Prince of Shiraz. Same age as Azizi – aged 22. Eldest son of the Sultan.

Faruq (pronounced *fa-rook*)

Meaning one who distinguishes truth from falsehood. Cousin to Ijlal, son of Giafar. A year older than Ijlal, aged 23

Husam (pronounced *hoo-sa-m*)

Meaning sword edge. He can express opinion with brutal honesty. Aged 21.

Fatin (pronounced *fa-teen*)

Intelligent and perceptive. Aged 19

Isamadeen (pronounced *isa-ma-deen*)

Twin brother to Rauf. His name means to guard. Always at attention, ready to pounce aged 20. He is the eldest of the twins, only by minutes, but he never lets Rauf forget this.

Rauf (pronounced *ra-oof*)

Gentle and kind, twin brother to Isamadeen, born a few minutes later. Aged 20

Jamal (pronounced *ja-māl*)

Means 'kind'. Similar personality to Rauf and just as michievous. Just turned aged 19

www.ingramcontent.com/pod-product-compliance
Lightning Source LLC
Chambersburg PA
CBHW061102100726
47911CB00012B/345

* 9 7 8 0 6 4 5 7 6 7 6 7 4 *